Innocent

SON

Carol Ferguson

AN INNOCENT SON
Copyright © 2008 Carol Ferguson

ISBN-10: 1-897373-52-X
ISBN-13: 978-1-897373-52-1

All rights reserved. No part of this publication may be reproduced, stored in a retrieval system, or transmitted in any form or by any means—electronic, mechanical, photocopy, recording, or any other—except for brief quotations in printed reviews, without the prior permission of the publisher.

This book is a work of fiction. Names, characters, places, and incidents are the product of the author's imagination or are used fictitiously. Any resemblance to actual events, locales, or persons, living or dead, is coincidental.

Printed by Word Alive Press
131 Cordite Road, Winnipeg, MB R3W 1S1
www.wordalivepress.ca

Acknowledgements

My first words of thanks must be to my Lord and Saviour, Jesus Christ, who calls, equips and finishes. Thank you to all the people who have urged me on in my writing and the writing groups who have shared their wisdom with me: Prairie Pens, InScribe, The Saskatchewan Writers Guild and Hillcrest Writer's Guild.

Words are not enough for those who did the awesome task of editing, but thank you: Larry Hadwen, Beth Byggdin, Pam Mytroen and my son-in-law, Cliff Reynolds. You were all wonderful in your honest advice, suggestions and encouragement.

My family is awesome and the love we all share is incredible. I am so glad each one is open, honest, forgiving and empathetic. I pray for each of you and for the generations that will follow after us. May those who follow after find us faithful.

This may sound strange, but thank you to the libraries, the Internet and all the people who provide amazing resources for people like me. How else could I write about a land I have never seen?

To those who read this book, may God wipe your tears and heal your wounds.

Carol Ferguson
May, 2008

An Innocent Son

✡ ✡ ✡

Chapter 1

JUDITH WAS FILLED with terror, running, hiding. She clutched something precious in her arms, but what was she protecting and why? Judith screamed.

"No! No! No!" Suddenly there was blood everywhere, on her hands, her clothing, the walls, the floor. Sobs shook her body.

"Judith!" Ethan's soothing voice penetrated her mind as his strong arms pulled her close to him, one hand stroked her back. "Wake up!"

Judith opened her eyes while her body still convulsed in sobs of grief.

"Was it a dream, Ethan? Was it just a bad nightmare?"

"No, it wasn't a dream." Judith could feel his tears join hers and run down her face. Then she remembered that precious joy that she tried to protect. Tried and failed.

Ten years earlier...

THE HAUNTING SOUND of the *shofer* echoed through the night silence. Judith's hands shook as she rolled off her mat and quickly dressed, fumbling with her veil. Her bridegroom was coming. It had been over a year since she stood with Ethan in this very room as their fathers arranged their marriage. She had fidgeted impatiently then, while the men conversed back and forth, working out the *mahar* that was being paid for her.

Up until that day she had been considered worthless, but when the *mahar*, was paid to her father, he in turn, gave some to her and for the first time in her life she was finally worth something. Some girls felt as if they were being bought, like a slave, but Judith felt none of that. Ethan's gifts were gifts of love. That was evident in *the matten,* gifts of coins and clothing, Ethan had presented to her. Judith had been relieved when all the conditions were finally worked out, and the betrothal contract, *shiyther erusin,* was signed.

"Blessed art Thou, Eternal our God, Creator of Heaven and Earth, who has given us the fruit of the vine. Amen." Judith recalled the love that filled her heart as Ethan raised the Cup of the Covenant he had so carefully poured. He drank from the cup and placed it in Judith's right hand. Judith sipped the wine never breaking eye contact with her beloved. It was the first time they had shared a cup and in that one action Judith accepted his love and protection. They were betrothed. Judith belonged to him and was thrilled at the glow in his eyes.

"I am returning to Bethlehem but I will come back for you as soon as our home is ready." Ethan left immediately.

Judith had gone for her purification bath with the words from the prophet Ezekiel running through her mind; *I entered into a covenant with thee and thou becamest Mine. Then I washed thee with water.* Although they were not yet officially married, this act designated a separation from her old life, to a new life and from then on Judith was veiled whenever she left the house. Ethan had come to visit her when he could but the time had been long. More than a year.

Now Judith shivered in delight as she pulled soft silky material over her head and felt it flow like a mist of water over her body. This was the wedding gown that Ethan had chosen for her. With trembling fingers she fastened a band of gold coins across her brow, another love offering from her groom.

Judith had known it would be a long betrothal. Ethan was preparing their home but in the end his father would decide when it was ready and Ethan could fetch his bride home. Moments ago when she heard the blowing of the shofer it was a surprise, expected and long awaited.

"Your bridegroom is coming." The shout from the other side of the house told her that her parents had heard it too. Suddenly the house was alive with activity. Almost everything was ready but it would still take time to gather all her belongings together. Ethan, like all bridegrooms was coming like a thief in the night, to steal her away, with her parents' permission, of course.

Hannah, her childhood friend was the first person in the door. Quickly she pulled the veil over Judith's face and tucked it in, leaving only her sparkling brown eyes exposed, peeking through the remaining slit, shining almost as brightly as the headband of gold coins.

Judith gasped in delight and her stomach gave an excited flip as her bridegroom strode into the room. Her legs felt weak. He was magnificent. Never before had she seen him dressed all in white and the robe was a sharp contrast to his beard and the riot of dark curls that wreathed his head. Judith took a long deep breath as he gazed about the room, searching for her. She hoped Ethan would be pleased with the choice of oils she had blended to rub into her skin, perfume that enveloped her now in a delicious scent. It was one of her gifts to him on their wedding day. Her sparkling dark eyes hinted at the huge smile that hid behind her embroidered veil.

Ethan spotted her, strolled confidently across the room and stopped in front of her. Slowly he stretched out his hand and with great ceremony lifted the veil and severely stared at her.

"She is the right one, yes?" Someone shouted.

Ethan's eyes twinkled. One eyebrow rose ever so slightly as he gazed into her eyes and teased her with his prolonged silence.

"That's her!" Applause and laughter erupted from their friends and family as he acknowledged her. The room rang with sudden chatter and backslapping. "I won't be tricked like Jacob was," Ethan remarked, referring to the story of Jacob in their ancient writings who, instead of marrying the love of his life, had been tricked by the veil into marrying her sister. What had once been a very serious matter had gradually evolved into a time of fun and teasing.

Every time Judith thought about that story she felt sorry for girls given in marriage to someone they hardly knew. Love would come later, people said, but Judith was glad love had come first for her. Ethan was so gentle. Every time he came he had a flower or a little gift for her. And he could make her laugh. She couldn't imagine the heartbreak she would feel if Ethan had taken the wrong girl and left her behind.

Silence fell like a blanket over the room, startling Judith out of her reverie. Gently, her father took her hand and placed it Ethan's hand, saying, "Take her! Take her home to your father's house with a good conscience. The God of heaven grant you a good journey in peace." Ethan gave her hand a soft squeeze and suddenly the place was full of noise, singing, laughter and jesting again, people bustling about, everyone trying to exit the house at once.

Judith took one last look around the home where she had grown up, etching a flood of memories in her mind. A single twinge of sadness shot through her as she mentally said good-bye to her childhood but her eyes brightened immediately as she envisioned her future with Ethan. Waiting until harvest was over, in addition to the entire year of betrothal seemed to have taken forever.

Hannah drew her close in a one-armed hug, balancing her curly-haired son on her hip. "So quickly the year has passed, hasn't it? And today a new life begins for you." When Hannah married Jacob and moved away to Bethlehem she talked often about her friend, Judith. Jacob's friend, Ethan, finally but quietly mentioned to his father that he would be interested in meeting Hannah's friend.

Now the two young women would be close to one another again.

"I'm so happy," Judith whispered, throwing her arms around Hannah, squeezing the toddler between them. The girls clung to each other until little Joatham protested. "You think we are going to smother you?" Judith laughed and ruffled the little one's hair. Judith gestured toward a young woman nearby, whose thickening waist indicated obvious signs of new life.

"I hope it will be soon for me too," she whispered with a grin. It was not only a dream of every Jewish girl, but also a duty to perpetuate her husband's family. Judith was aware of the huge responsibility she would carry. Ethan was an only child.

A boisterous crowd of friends and family filled the road to Ethan's home in Bethlehem. Judith's girlfriends rhythmically banged tambourines on their hips, their heads and their hands as the crowd started down the winding path. Young men carried all Judith's earthly belongings on their shoulders. Even her grandmother's cooking pots, which had been passed on to Judith, seemed to bang in time to the music. The morning sunrise cast a rosy glow on the red-earthed hills. *Just like the glow in my heart,* Judith thought.

Harvested fields fanned out on one side of them. On the other side, feathery leaves of the olive trees quivered in the breeze. Judith could just pick out signs of new fruit. *This year I will be picking and pressing olive in my own home.* A shiver of anticipation welled up inside her.

Sparrows flitted about as if they were a part of the procession. Finches and larks sang the songs that were in

Judith's heart and shepherds, leading their flocks to pasture across the rocky terrain, shouted blessings on the bridal pair.

As they entered Bethlehem Judith eagerly looked forward to seeing the haven Ethan had prepared for her, an addition to his parents' home. She just knew it would contain all kinds of unique gestures of his love. *Jehovah is smiling on us today.*

Judith glanced around as her stomach rumbled. Standing straighter, she tightened her stomach muscles to quiet the pangs of hunger, and maintain a dignified demeanor to go along with her wedding finery. Her hand flew to her mouth to suppress a giggle, making the gold bracelets on her arm jingle. Then she chuckled. No one could hear her stomach above the laughter and singing. Ethan's stomach was probably growling too, since he had fasted the previous day in preparation for this great event.

Ethan's hand brushed across hers in a touch of affection. "We're almost there." In keeping with the Law, they had not seen each other for the past seven days, not until the moment Ethan lifted her veil.

Judith thought about the young brides she had seen weep through their wedding day. She and Ethan exchanged glances. He was watching her every move and expression and she was far from crying.

A gentle breeze ruffled the fringe on the huppah held aloft by four corner poles, creating an intimate, secure place for them in the walled yard of his parents home. The crowd buzzed around and finally quieted as Judith joined Ethan under the prayer canopy. Friends read the *sheva brachos,* seven special wedding blessings. As often as she had heard these blessings recited they had never before impacted her heart and mind. Today they sent joy through her soul.

"Yes!" She agreed, as the first blessing, recited over a full cup of wine, praised God for His entire creation. The next blessing praised Him for the creation of the human being, and the third for the creation of the human as a *two part creature,* woman and man and that Ethan and Judith would rejoice together forever, like Adam and Eve. Judith echoed that praise as she glanced at her handsome groom. The last three blessings were for Jerusalem, the Temple and the Jewish people. Judith had never felt so blessed. *I can hardly wait to see how Jehovah brings that about in our lives.*

A first cup of wine had been a part of their betrothal, over a year ago. Now, finally, the second cup of wine was drunk, sealing their marriage covenant. The laughter and fun carried on until the bridal couple slipped away from the gathering and Judith finally saw the place Ethan had prepared for her. As an unmarried couple they had never been allowed to be alone so when Jacob as their witness ushered them into the new addition, it was a sign to everyone that they were really married. The door closed and for the first time ever, they were alone.

"I've missed you," Ethan whispered in Judith's ear. He gently removed her veil and brushed his hand over her cheek. The Law had restricted their intimacy to this point and now Ethan couldn't get enough of the softness of her skin the silkiness of her hair. Lifting her hand, he brought her fingers to his face.

Judith felt his beard, surprised that it wasn't prickly like she imagined. She ran her fingers across the bridge of his nose. A shiver bounced down Judith's spine as Ethan brushed his thumb across her lips. He lifted one eyebrow.

Judith laughed. "I love it when you do that."

"I know." Ethan wiggled his eyebrow up and down. "For a year I have been watching your response to that little twitch. You have some little gestures that bring out a response in me too, and a lifetime to discover what they are." Ethan drew Judith into his arms and feathered kisses across her face and finally found her lips. "I've waited so long to do this. But I'm starving."

Judith searched through the abundance of food that had been provided for the seven days and nights they would be sequestered here together.

"Come and eat." Finally, she had the privilege of ministering to Ethan's needs. She fed him grapes fresh from the vine, along with cheese, almonds and date cakes, refilling his plate over and over with things she knew he liked. Feeling completely at home with each other they lingered over every morsel of food, teasing each other, tossing grapes into open mouths, every gesture oozing with love. They could hear their friends leaving for their own homes, but knew they would return for the wedding feast at the end of the seven days.

Silence finally reigned over the entire building and the bridal couple was oblivious of what went on outside their door as the marriage bed beckoned to them.

During those seven days Judith had never felt so loved. She had never laughed so much as they shared the stories of their lives. Ethan took the time to quietly set aside a bundle of bed linen, important evidence that Judith had come to him as a chaste bride.

They dreamed together of the future and laid down a strong foundation that would stand firm throughout the years ahead. Every once in a while Judith would hear the strident voice of Ethan's mother, raised in anger in another part of the house. Ethan was quick to muffle the sound by beginning a story or a song. Sometimes in the dark of night, Judith wondered what her life would be like, living and working with her mother-in-law.

"I don't think we can delay any longer, *bubeleh*, sweetheart." Ethan finally stated on the seventh day as they began to hear sounds of music and laughter as their friends and family gathered once more. "Our friends, God forbid, will soon be breaking down the door."

"Then, my dear husband, let's go celebrate!" Judith grabbed Ethan's hand and together they joined the crowd already well into the revelry. Toes tapped as music filled the room.

"Come! Dance!" someone shouted. Judith kicked off her sandals, linked arms with the women and soon they were spinning about the room, feet flashing, skirts swirling. The slap of bare feet on the floor kept perfect time with the music as they dipped, twirled, clapped and danced. The men, in a circle around the girls, jumped and kicked higher and higher, the muscles in their legs taking the strain of crouches and leaps. Each dance became faster and louder, heels drumming rhythmically on the floor until the room was hot and humid from all the activity.

With every spin around the floor, Judith caught Ethan's eye and laughed as he raised an eyebrow.

"Enough! Enough!" Ethan's mother clapped her hands and the music ground to a halt. "Enough dancing for now.

The marriage banquet is waiting. Eat, everyone!" The elaborate feast left everyone groaning in satisfaction.

"This is only the beginning," Ethan's friend Jacob gave him a friendly nudge. "We will continue to pray blessings on your marriage."

The crowd was still full of energy as they took their leave. It had been the most wonderful week of Judith's life. Only one thing could add more joy to her life - a child this time next year.

They had been created for one another and together they would keep The Law. She would be a good wife and daughter-in-law. She and Ethan had their own room but it soon became very clear that it was not her home.

Chapter 2

"You have a strong back, yes? You can fetch the water. I'm getting too old for that. I'll go to the market while you clean up after the meal. You know how to grind barley, yes? The barley is in the courtyard. So is the olive press. You know how to press olives, yes? You will do that too!" Ayla laid down an agenda the first chance she had.

Judith bit her lip to hold back a laugh. *She must think she gained a donkey when Ethan got married.* Her own mother had trained Judith well. She had beautiful memories of talking and laughing together as they worked, and envisioned working together with her new mother-in-law. But she certainly hadn't imagined that *all* the work in this home would fall on her. Maybe, she thought, Ayla was joking, bringing some levity into their relationship. The older woman stared at Judith. It was evident that she wasn't joking. Judith had just been given a full-time job. It was the olive press she was most apprehensive about.

Judith woke slowly the next morning with Ethan's arm holding her, snuggled spoon fashion against him. The small house was chilly. She smothered her giggles so his parents wouldn't hear as Ethan whispered and teased, holding her close, pushing his nose into her ear. Finally, wishing she could stay right where she was, she reluctantly forced herself to leave the warmth of their bed and put fresh kindling on the fire to warm the house and heat the oven to bake the daily supply of barley loaves.

Soon the delicious aroma of freshly baked barley loaves had Ethan prowling around, easily distracting Judith with hugs and kisses before his parents finally appeared. Judith placed the fruit, cheese, and cooling loaves on the table.

Noam offered *motzi*, a melodic blessing for the food. *Blessed art thou, O, Lord, our God, King of the universe, who causes to come forth bread from the earth.*

Ethan helped himself to the fresh bread, enjoying its warmth as he held it in his hand, proud that his beloved wife could make such delicate loaves. He gave his mother a proud look of satisfaction as he stuffed a morsel into his mouth and reached for the cheese. A strange look passed over his face as he slowly chewed and swallowed. His father took a bite of bread and the men exchanged glances.

Judith looked from one to the other, waiting for words of praise that didn't come. These loaves were perfect, the best and lightest she had ever made. She watched Ethan chew on his lower lip, biting back the hint of a grin while his father covered his mouth and coughed several times.

Ayla, her mother-in-law, bit into a piece of bread and spat it out on the floor. "Yeach! You don't know to put salt in the bread dough?" the older woman asked gruffly. "This is only fit to feed to the dogs." Jumping up the woman began gathering up all the bread.

Judith dutifully rose to help, avoiding eye contact with everyone, even Ethan. She couldn't believe it. All the times she had made bread at home she had never forgotten to add salt.

"Leave it!" Ethan's father stated bluntly. "It won't hurt us to eat unsalted bread. Is it not right that every bride make a mistake or two?" His wife dumped the bread back onto the table and sat down abruptly, her face flushed as her husband stared at her. There was absolute silence. Nobody moved as Noam stared at his wife and she defiantly stared back. Judith held her breath. The foursome was frozen in a moment that went on and on. Finally, Ayla looked away and the tension was broken.

"It's all right," Ethan pulled Judith back down onto the bench beside him. "Except for the salt, they are very nice loaves."

Judith's heart flooded with love for such an understanding husband. She loved being his wife but she didn't love being Ayla's daughter-in-law! Judith sat hunched over in humiliation as Ethan intoned the benedictions that ended each meal. She didn't even hear him thank God who provided bread, blessed the land that produced the food or praise God for his love and kindness. She was just thankful the meal was over as he closed with verses from the Psalms and a prayer for peace.

For such a wonderful man I am determined to do my best to keep peace in this home, Judith thought later as she dug a hole and buried the remainder of the bread. The scathing words of her mother-in-law made her determined to never make that mistake again but, along with the tasteless bread, she buried her dream of working side-by-side with a loving mother-in-law.

Since her first bungled morning she and Ethan played a silent game every time she brought fresh steaming loaves to the table. As his parents concentrated on their meal, Ethan rolled his eyes in ecstasy and lifted an eyebrow as he took his first bite. Judith watched in delight, a tiny grin hovering at the corners of her mouth before rushing back to her work.

✡ ✡ ✡

"ROSH HASHANAH WILL be our first festival as husband and wife," Ethan whispered into Judith's thick hair as they cuddled in bed. "This will be a new year for us together too."

"I love hearing the story of Abraham and Isaac and the blowing of the *shofar*. I'll help your mother make the honey cakes," Judith said with excitement, "or maybe I'll make them myself." *I'll prove to Ethan's mother that I am a good wife.*

"I'm ploughing today," Ethan stated at the breakfast table. "So the fields will be ready for the next planting."

"I could bring your noon meal to you," Judith stated eagerly.

"You want to waste our time with that?" His mother scoffed. Ethan grinned at Judith behind his mother's back and before the men finished their meal that morning, the woman had loaves and cheese wrapped for the men to take with their water bags. Noam would be taking their flock of sheep to pasture as he did every day.

"I'll miss you," Ethan whispered in her ear as he left, turning around to return Judith's wave.

When Ayla finally left for the market, Judith moved with a lighter step and a song issued softly from her lips as she washed and stored the dairy dishes and utensils in a separate area from those used for meat. By law the two food items could never be served at the same meal nor could the designated dishes ever come in contact with one another. For that reason, they seldom ate meat. Judith obeyed all the kosher laws and would not risk a scolding from Ethan's mother. More important, she would do nothing to offend her God.

Judith breathed deeply as she finally stepped outside, her work finished. The small leather pail for dipping water slapped against her hip as she hurried up the steps hewn into the rocky slopes of the village, her water pot balanced on her head. The day was crisp and fresh and young girls chattered and laughed as they walked to the well, their sandaled feet snapping on the hard packed path. Judith had been quickly welcomed into the younger community.

"How is the bride today?" Judith's new friends exchanged sly glances and giggles as they lowered their veils and clustered around the well, dipping up water. "Anything new to report?" This was the place where the women exchanged local gossip and ideas every day while the men gathered at the city gates to hear news from far away.

Judith tried hard to think of a reply, knowing there was more behind the question than politeness. Sometimes she wondered why they didn't just ask the question outright. They made her felt like a bride, even now, months after her marriage. *They've probably been counting the months on their fingers, just waiting for the first sign of a baby.* It had been half a year since their marriage. Those who were obviously with child strutted proudly around her.

"That the Lord would be so good to me," Judith finally responded with a smile. It was always safest to put the oness on the creator of life. She was relieved when, as expected, their chatter moved on to other topics. Each sickness that appeared was discussed and various cures from generations past were shared, each family claiming the ultimate remedy. They rehashed village news and talked over every aspect of housekeeping. Today the major topic was the rancid cheese someone had purchased from the cheesemaker.

"That man knows nothing," someone stated.

Here at the well, Judith told the embarrassing story of her unsalted bread. Her story elicited details from almost every one of them, describing an unmarked grave near their homes where they, too, had buried a batch of bread

Judith watched and listened and soon realized, though no one spoke of it directly, that there were several young women living with their mothers-in-law and enduring the same suffering. They shared ideas and occasionally even tears. Gently they soothed each others bruised hearts. Judith's heart went out to a young girl her own age, also newly married, but to a man who took his mother's side at every opportunity.

Judith had quickly felt safety among her peers and freedom to join in the discussions. The young women in the small village were a close knit group but Hannah was the one she really confided in. Together they teased each other and fussed with Hannah's little Joatham. Judith's eyes glowed as she nuzzled the chubby babe.

"A new tooth it is that hurts him." Hannah explained away the rosy cheeks and warm forehead. "Someday you'll have the joy of a fussy baby keeping you awake too," she teased. "You'll become friends with every star in the sky."

Judith reluctantly returned the baby to his mother and hoisted her water jar onto her shoulder. Ayla would be wondering what took her so long. Their home consisted of only two rooms off the living area and a courtyard so the young couple had little privacy and when the two women were home together Judith had no privacy at all. She often wished she had the nerve to just go into her own room and stay there until the men came home. Secretly, she was glad there was no space to build another room. When their own family began to grow, they would need to find a home of their own.

Now, as the afternoon faded away, Judith picked up the small straw broom they used to sweep the hard clay floors. Quickly she swept around the hearth. She swept closer and closer to the window as evening approached. The one small window overlooked green fields and olive groves. Judith glanced out the window as she swept, trying to hide her eagerness from her observant mother-in-law.

Daily, Judith praised Jehovah that the house stood on the edge of Bethlehem, perched on a low, but steep ridge in the rocky hills of Judea. From here she could watch for the flock to come down the hill. The sheepfold, a cavern in the hill, was actually the lower portion of the house. Approaching from town, no one would realize the sheep bedded down below them, yet it was very convenient. If

Ethan's mother ever wondered why one area of the house got so much attention in the late afternoon, she never said.

Today, Judith spied the men as they came over the hill with the flock and began to count. If she wasn't interrupted, she could calculate almost the exact time it took Ethan and his father to climb the steep rocky path up to the house. They would step through the door, reciting *broche,* a short prayer of praise always said before they began their ritualistic hand washing. It was also the first thing said in the morning and the last at night, and at every new season, new moon or the acquisition of a new garment.

Judith scurried into the courtyard and busied herself knowing Ethan would come looking for her. Words of praise would also be the first thing out of Ethan's mouth when he laid eyes on Judith.

Chapter 3

MINUTES LATER, ETHAN'S loud whisper, "Judith!" preceded him through the courtyard door. Judith would be waiting behind the door with a grin on her face, reveling in this little ritual they observed every day. He loved how she threw herself into his arms as soon as he appeared. He had no doubt she was in great need of a hug. Lifting her off her feet he swung her around as their lips met. As usual, Ayla came trudging after him, complaining about one thing or another, and Ethan quickly released his wife.

Every day was the same until one day Ethan backed up against the door with Judith in his arms. He kissed her and nuzzled her neck while his mother demanded that he open the door so she could get something or other from the courtyard. The ensuing tongue-lashing wasn't worth trying that again, but even so, the atmosphere in the house lightened when the men arrived.

Judith felt sorry for Noam. He was the most gentle, caring man. Had his wife ever kissed him? She could hardly picture Ayla young and in love. Had she been? In love at one time? Was it possible that Ayla had been given in marriage to a man she didn't know and didn't want? Who could not love Noam? He was a mature picture of Ethan. Judith wondered if Ayla was jealous because she and Ethan were so much in love.

The time of the olive harvest arrived and Judith approached the event with fear. The olives were not difficult to pick; they almost fell off the tree when they were ripe. Even pitting them wasn't so bad. This was one of the many jobs Ayla had foisted onto Judith. A large stone bowl-shaped basin waited for the pitted olives and once they were in that basin, another stone sitting upright on its side, with a large wooden stick through its center hole, was used to press the oil from the olives. Judith's back almost ached just thinking about it.

Judith put all her weight into the job as she rolled the stone around and around the basin. As the oil poured into one container, she placed the crushed pulp into a woven bag to be pressed again. This first pressing produced pure oil for their lamps and ointments. Then she would press the pulp again and again until there was no oil left to extract.

Spring arrived with spring lambs and new growth all around the countryside put a new longing within Judith for a baby. Ayla did little around the house other than provide constant and unwelcome advice, so Judith even relished the job of going out to find dried dung to burn in the fire - a thankless job but anything that got her outside in the fresh spring air was welcome.

Judith took a deep breath as she walked out the door with her woven bag. The sun was bright and the hills glowed in rich earth tones. Judith carefully gathered her load, kicking at the dung to make sure it was dry before she picked it up. She watched the lambs leaping and playing tag as she made her way across the hills. She dawdled and then tried to look surprised when Ethan and Noam came over the hill with the flock. She looked forward to walking home with them.

"I will take the flock home," Noam told them with a grin. "You two be alone together. A blessing on your heads."

Judith left her bag of chips and ran over the hills with Ethan, gathering flowers and feeling like a newborn lamb herself. Noam's name meant *friendship* and today Judith saw him not only as her father-in-law, but also as her friend.

"It's been months since I've felt so alive," Judith stated as she sat with Ethan on the top of a hill while he guided her through the finer details of using a sling.

"You have been under my mother's thumb for months," Ethan replied. "I know what goes on between the two of you, Judith." He put a stone in the sling and positioned Judith's hands.

"Do you think she's jealous of us? Do you think she ever loved your father as much as I love you?" She swung the sling and laughed when the stone landed a short distance away. "I don't want to turn out like that in my old age."

"As if you ever could," Ethan laughed. "So tell me something new."

"I think I might be with child!" She enjoyed Ethan's quick hug and snuggled against him. They dreamed and planned for the future as they continued to wander across the hills. But, two days later Judith realized there would be no baby. Disappointed, she went for her ritual bath that month and the month after that.

"Tomorrow we will shear the sheep. Do you want to come and help?" Ethan did all the shearing of their fat-tailed sheep, as Noam was finding the bending too painful for his aging body.

"Do I want to come and help?" Judith threw her arms around Ethan's neck, glad they were in a private place just then. She would be outside and away from Ayla for the whole day and she danced around the room with joy.

The next morning they went down early to the sheepcote and Ethan had several sheep sheared before the sun grew warm. As the sun got hotter he pulled his arms out of his tunic and left it hanging around his waist, leaving his upper body bare. The ripple of muscles as he worked had Judith mesmerized. She watched a bead of sweat glisten and run down his back as he flipped a sheep onto its tailbone and ran the shears in long firm strokes down the ewe's chest towards her belly.

The belly fleece dropped onto the ground as he sheared out from the belly and up the flank. Ethan's movements were fluid and gentle. He dipped the shears in water when the lanolin built up. Judith marveled at how docile the ewes were during the shearing. They were absolutely silent and never struggled to escape. Judith could understand that. She would never struggle to escape Ethan either.

Gently the shears moved across the sheep's cheek and down one side of the neck then across the other side of the face. Ethan manipulated the shears over the shoulder and onto the final leg. Finally, the last of the fleece was free and he released the naked, bewildered ewe.

"Judith, are you dreaming?" Ethan stood gazing at her, waiting for her to roll up the fleece.

Judith shook herself awake, finally tearing her attention away from the curly hair on his chest. She laughed at the stark creature he had just sheared and quickly she rolled the fleece. Then she refrained from looking at Ethan's bare chest again.

Although their flock was not a large one, it took several days to do the shearing. Ethan's father always had another ewe ready and waiting for the shears.

"We have another profitable year ahead." Judith said, looking over the results of their efforts. In the past, Ethan and Noam sold all the fleeces because Ayla couldn't be bothered with the work that went with weaving, including the washing of all the fleeces. "I'll be able to do lots of weaving judging from the piles of fleece."

Judith took the pile to a nearby stream, and using lye soap Ayla had made, she washed away all the dirt and extra oils. Judith loved weaving. She thought about what she would make as she beat out the excess water from the soggy fleece. Then she laid them out on the rocks to dry in the sun. She loved watching garments and robes come into being. But most of all, she loved experimenting with colors. Looking at the tangled wool spread out before her, she knew that she would turn their own wool into a lucrative business. She squeezed the wool, feeling the rich oils that gave it quality.

"Sometime we'll have to get a proper loom set up for you," Ethan stated days later as he helped Judith carry the fleece home.

Judith smiled at the thought. She sat on the floor to weave now, with the yarn tied to stakes pounded into the floor. It was an arrangement that didn't take up much space and even Ayla couldn't complain that she was in the way.

"A loom would be wonderful but we have no room for one in such a small house, yes? Weaving on the floor takes up less space." It was something else to add to her list of dreams, though.

"HANNAH IS AVOIDING ME," Judith declared when another year had passed with no increase in their family. She was sorting her skeins of wool while Ethan relaxed in the courtyard beside her, one of their few private moments. "I know why, too. She has another baby and she feels sorry for me." Hannah's baby girl, Tirzah, was a month old. In spite of the ache in her heart, Judith had woven a soft blanket for the new baby but she had seldom seen her friend since the day she had taken the blanket to her.

"I don't think so." Ethan continued the conversation. "Maybe she's not feeling well. Maybe she is chasing Joatham, who runs around now."

Judith was disappointed that for them there was no sign of a baby yet and Ethan's mother was running out of patience.

Almost monthly she asked sarcastically, "You are giving us a grandchild, yes?"

"No! Not yet. Someday, Jehovah willing," Judith always answered. How could Ayla argue if it was Jehovah's problem?

"You produce only robes and blankets while other young women produce babies! Sons!" That remark was accompanied by a sneer.

A tear rolled down Judith's cheek but she stiffened her back and went on with her work. In her heart Judith whispered a silent prayer for a speedy answer.

Ethan, on the other hand, found time to walk alone in the hills and beseech Jehovah for a child. If Noam ever wondered why his son disappeared at times, he never mentioned it.

Every month Judith made the trek through the village for her ritual purification baths. Veil over her face, head down, Judith felt as if everyone in the village was watching and sneering.

This is one of the few things I can thank the Romans for, she often thought as she bathed, *building viaducts to bring fresh water to Bethlehem from the gulf. It's the only good thing I can say about them.* If her monthly cycle was late, Judith was full of hope, only to fall into depths of despair when it resumed. All the while she became more vigilant then ever about obeying all the law. Even the traditions of the fathers, passed down by word of mouth, she followed explicitly.

Judith expanded the weaving part of the family business a bit more and buried herself in making woolen garments. She filled her time combing, spinning and dyeing wool. The hearth in the courtyard was useful for heating water for dye baths and kept the small house from becoming hot and humid.

"You think I should start selling our robes and blankets in Jerusalem?" Judith asked Ethan one day when she was feeling unusually frustrated with her barrenness. "We could go early for the feast days and set up a booth."

"From your mouth to God's ears," Ethan responded. "People will pay a good price for the robes and blankets you make."

Perhaps I can also go to the temple to pray, like Hannah, Samuel's mother, Judith thought, but she would never suggest such a thing to Ethan. Could a man ever understand the frustration a barren woman felt? Thus began their business trips to Jerusalem to sell her crafts. She planned and prepared for each trip with enthusiasm but always there was the emptiness and the question. *What have we done wrong?*

✡ ✡ ✡

"ARE YOU HUNGRY?" Judith knelt on the sleeping mat where Ethan lay on his stomach, dozing. He had been out most of the night looking after an injured ram. Planting a kiss on his neck she kneaded his shoulder muscles until a groan of bliss indicated that he was awake. "Come, eat a little something!"

"Where are my parents?" Ethan asked sleepily.

"Your mother has gone to the market and your father has taken the rest of the flock to the pasture."

Ethan rolled over and lunged for her but Judith jumped, avoiding his grasp, and ran laughing from the room. Within minutes she felt Ethan come up behind her where she knelt by the hearth and wrap his arms around her.

"Ethan, Stop! You want I should drop the bowl?" she scolded quietly. The pottery, decorated with colored circles and squares, was a gift from Hannah. Her husband, Jacob, was Ethan's close friend and the village potter. Judith used the beautiful pottery daily but with great care. "What would I say to Jacob if I broke his pottery?"

"Oh, it is Jacob's pottery? I thought Hannah gave it to you," Ethan said, tickling her so she almost dropped it again.

"Sit down and behave yourself!" Judith's smiling face took the sting out of the command. "How is the injured ram?"

"I think he'll be fine but he can't go out to the pasture for a few days." Ethan sat down, noting her high spirits. "What has you so full of life today? You have discovered some new dye for your wool, yes?"

"Jehovah has blessed me beyond that." Her hand unconsciously flattened across her stomach. Judith's eyes twinkled. She grinned at the incredulous look on Ethan's face.

Chapter 4

"OH, ETHAN. FINALLY, we're going to have a baby. We've waited four long years." This time there was no doubt.

"A baby?" Ethan grabbed her in a hug, twirling her around and around the room. Then just as quickly he let her go. "Oh, I'm sorry. I shouldn't be so rough."

"We need to go immediately to the Temple in Jerusalem and give praise to Jehovah. Can you walk that far? Do you want to ride on the donkey?" Ethan paced back and forth in the room as he made plans for the trip to Jerusalem.

Ethan's father was overjoyed to hear their news; his mother huffed and muttered that it was about time.

The path seemed smoother, the sun brighter as they made their joyful journey to Jerusalem. Ethan danced circles around his wife, clapping and singing to entertain her. Judith had no need to be entertained.

"What nonsense," she chided him. But her heart was at peace at last and full of love for this man who was acting so silly. *It should be me jumping around and acting like a spring lamb.*

After their trip to Jerusalem, another plan began to take shape in Ethan's mind. He had not been blind to the friction between his wife and his mother, although the older woman was a bit more accepting now that a baby was on the way. They needed a home of their own. He kept his thoughts a secret from Judith in case nothing came of it, sharing his desire only with his father.

Months passed before Noam heard of a man who had moved his family into a larger house. Their vacated building was small, two rooms and a courtyard, even smaller than the home his parents owned. Ethan quickly made arrangements to buy it.

Judith was concentrating on the wonderful fact that they were at last going to have a baby. She thrilled to the movement in her womb as the baby kicked and rolled. She failed to notice the quiet talks Ethan and Noam shared or that Ethan headed a different direction when he left the house.

First Ethan covered the mud brick walls of the tiny house with a fresh mixture of mud, dung and straw. While that dried, Ethan laid a clean layer of clay in the courtyard, making it smooth and comfortable to walk on.

"I'm becoming quite good at sneaking around," he laughed to himself one day, as he narrowly missed running into Judith on her way to the well. He was glad that everyone in the village had entered into his game and kept the secret. Some of their friends even left the occasional jar of water for him.

Judith's brow wrinkled in puzzlement as she walked through the village one day on her way to the well. "That sounds like Ethan singing," she thought. She paused and shook her head. "But he's out with the sheep today." As she neared a small vacant house the singing became more distinct. It did sound like Ethan! Judith tiptoed closer and peeked into the small dwelling. It was Ethan. He was on his hands and knees in the courtyard carefully digging stones from the clay floor. Why? Silently, puzzled, Judith stood and watched him.

Ethan looked up and a huge smile creased his face. "What do you think of it?" He jumped to his feet and came toward her his hands caked with clay. Playfully he reached out to touch her cheek.

"What do I think of it? What are you doing here?" Judith darted out of his reach. "Stay away with your dirty hands. You are helping someone with their work?"

"It's a surprise for you." Ethan wrapped his arms around Judith, taking care to keep his clay-covered hands off her. Their baby, nestled in Judith's womb, came gently between them. "This is our new home," he told her quietly. "I hope you like it."

Judith was speechless as Ethan showed her around the dwelling. She quickly realized he had been removing pebbles where tiny knees could get skinned in the years ahead. Her heart swelled with love for this thoughtful man. Walking around, she saw the future. Here, she would cook their meals, there, she would weave.

Ethan was delighted with the look of joy on her face. Her kisses and hugs only added to his happiness. "This is going to be a wonderful home for our baby," he stated. "A place of peace and joy." Together, they wandered through the small dwelling planning where their belongings would fit.

"You are moving?" Ayla screeched. She too, had been kept in the dark but for different reasons. "You have no concern for your aging parents?" she raged. "What is to become of us?"

"I have talked to your sister," Noam informed his wife. "Her daughter, Nina, is a widow and needs a place to live. She will live with us and help you."

"Just like that you arrange my life? Thank you for nothing! Let her come. Maybe I won't like her. And just because a woman gives birth to a baby doesn't mean she'll raise him!"

Judith took to stopping in every day to watch Ethan finish the house. She was amazed at the time he spent on every little detail. Nothing escaped his careful attention. Spending time alone, being able to talk freely to one another was a delight to her. "Ethan, what did your mother mean when she said just because you have a baby doesn't mean you'll raise him?"

"I wasn't their only child," he replied. "My mother gave birth to one baby after another only to have them die as infants. No one knows why I alone lived."

Judith suddenly realized why Ayla was so bitter. The thought of losing her baby even after it was born was a horrible thought.

Ethan, recognizing the darkness that had settled over her mind, soon had her concentrating on their new home again. He knew this was a dream come true for Judith. Just one of her many dreams she had shared with him. Finally, he could give her freedom.

Ayla let Judith know in various ways that she disapproved of their move. She kept her rude remarks for when

Ethan was away from the house but was kindness personified when her son was around.

"How many years have I waited for a grandchild? Now you are taking it away from me before it ever sees the light of day. What kind of a daughter would do that?" Ayla's name meant *oak tree* and Judith often saw the woman's strength, but now she saw the pain behind her angry words.

Nina moved in to live with Ethan's parents the day Judith and Ethan moved out. Judith knew immediately that the old woman's wrath would be poured out on the niece and felt a real sympathy for her.

Judith was in her seventh month, heavy and uncomfortable, when they moved. It was a happy day, marred only by Ayla's gloomy attitude. "Leave me in peace," was her parting remark. Finally Judith could hang up the copper pots that had once belonged to her grandmother.

"You want me to put up some shelves for the dishes and utensils?" Ethan asked. As soon as Judith made her decision he built them. Ethan was quick to add whatever conveniences she wanted.

"You have no place to hang bags," he said, glancing around. "Some pegs you need, yes?" He bored holes and inserted pegs in the upper portion of the poles that supported the roof and then watched as Judith hung his outer garment on the peg closest to the door and woven bags on the other hooks. He loved to please his wife and she was so easy to please.

"What do I do with this?" Ethan asked, as the evening grew dark. He was holding the lamp, with nowhere to set it down. "Am I meant to be a lamp stand forever?"

Judith laughed and took the lamp, setting it on the floor. The next day Ethan carved several niches into the walls where the lamp could sit, casting its warm glow over their evening work. Judith fussed over the dishes, arranging them just so on the shelves. She swept the clay floors continually and cleaned the hearth even when pregnancy made bending and lifting difficult.

"Let me rub your back," Ethan whispered at night when Judith couldn't find any position that was comfortable.

"You should be sleeping," Judith murmured. "I'm sorry I woke you. I didn't realize all this extra weight would make me so tired. Look at me; I'm just one huge swollen lump!"

"It's the heat," Ethan replied, massaging her back muscles. "Besides, you're a beautiful lump."

Judith playfully shoved him away but soon his hands were working their comfort again, gradually slowing and then stopping when she finally fell asleep. During the day Judith appreciated the shade of the partially covered inner courtyard. She sat whenever her chores allowed, her swollen ankles propped on a jar.

"So how come no one ever tells you how it feels to be pregnant?" Judith grumbled one day.

"I don't know," Ethan replied, his eye twinkling. "You think I should know about being pregnant? You tell me. What is it like?"

"It is a joyous time, but I have no energy to rejoice. So many things I want to get ready for the baby, but I can barely get my daily work done. I am waiting for the birth, but I'm frightened. I keep thinking about your mother."

"Jehovah will strengthen you," Ethan reassured her.

Rainy days brought a bit of relief from the heat, and then she appreciated the covered portion of the courtyard because she could hang wet clothes or skeins of yarn to dry. On those days she used the small hearth inside for cooking.

Judith often saw Nina at the well. She tried to draw the woman into conversation but Nina was a reserved person, never complaining about her aunt, seemingly content with what life had dealt her. Other women chattered all around them, their questions and insults having stopped as soon as Judith's pregnancy became evident.

"Hurry has a new meaning for me now," she told Hannah with a grin as they worked side by side at the well filling their water jugs. Judith was breathless as she bent over the well. "You can't go very fast when you waddle."

"Come and visit me," Hannah suggested. "We haven't had a chance to visit much lately. You can see Jacob's new lamps."

Judith finished her morning chores and plodded her way to Hannah's home. Bypassing the house she entered the out-building that housed Jacob's pottery. Hannah was busy rearranging the vast amount of pottery that Jacob was preparing to take to Jerusalem to sell. Moving her bulk gingerly to avoid knocking over piles of pottery, Judith walked between the rows. The laughter of Hannah's children delighted Judith's heart as they played outside the door. Joatham bravely scampered along the top of the short wall surrounding the home. She gazed at shelf after shelf displaying Jacob's talent.

"What are these?" Judith asked, picking up what looked like a cast off piece of clay. "Did Jacob make this many mistakes on his potter's wheel?"

"Those are for a loom. Weights to hold down the strands of wool during weaving. Look at the lamps Jacob has finished. Here's one that matches the pottery I gave you."

"How beautiful," Judith caressed the smooth oval-shaped lamp. "I had no idea Jacob had so many things made. Such a wonderful selection. We really do need a second lamp," Judith admitted. "Ethan has the lantern to use when he's out with the sheep at night but it would be nice to have a second lamp when we're at home working in different rooms." Tucking her finger into the handle of several lamps, she searched for one that could accommodate Ethan's larger fingers. The lid that covered the oil chamber opened easily. She poked at the protrusion on the opposite side, where the wick nestled. Judith was not one to make a hasty decision and the heat from Jacob's kiln soon had the sweat running down Judith's neck as she deliberated.

"I'll take this one," she finally said. "Maybe someday we'll even need to buy another one." Hannah carefully wrapped a cloth about the breakable object. Clutching her purchase carefully, Judith hurried home as fast as her bulk would allow. The cooing of doves turned her mind to thinking of the birds being raised to be sold for sacrifice in the temple.

"When our child arrives, Ethan will buy a dove and take it, together with one of our lambs, to the temple for a sacrifice. Please, Jehovah, make it soon."

The clatter of mauls on copper could be heard in the distance where coppersmiths continued their age-old trade. Hammering sounds came, as usual, from the home of the local carpenter who supplied the townspeople with plows, looms and furniture.

"Someday we'll order more benches and chests. Some day," and her dreams filled her thoughts as she walked in the warm sun. She didn't notice Ethan come from the home of the carpenter.

Chapter 5

ETHAN HURRIED TO catch up to her, unable to keep his excitement to himself. Judith jumped as his voice brought her out of her dream.

"Ethan! You scared me. What are you doing here?"

"It's hard for you to sit on the floor to weave, yes?" Ethan stated. "I promised you a loom a long time ago. Now it's time. The carpenter has been helping me cut the pieces for your new loom."

"My own loom?" Judith was almost speechless. "That I am so blessed. Think of all the weaving I can do. I'm preparing the wool to start on an exceptionally fine shawl for the baby, even nicer than the ones I made for Hannah. It will be the first thing I'll weave on the new loom."

She pulled Ethan through the door when they arrived home, hardly giving him a chance to duck and avoid hitting his head on the low lintel. "I know just where to put it." Judith indicated a corner of the second room, a room that held only a single chest where they stored clothing and sleeping mats. "Right here!" Ethan looked over the area, pacing off the length.

"I think I could fasten the cross beam of the loom right here," he held his hand at a height that he knew Judith would be able to reach when she was ready to work. "And the tunnel you slide the shuttle through, that you call a *shed*, would be about here. Or would you rather have the loom up on the roof?"

"What? You want me to be running up and down the stairs to stay slim?" Judith said with a twinkle in her eye. "That would be too inconvenient when the baby comes. This will be perfect. I'll be away from the weather in the rainy seasons and it stays cool in here at other times." Ethan couldn't resist Judith's enthusiasm.

Ethan still helped with the flock every morning but Noam took the sheep to pasture each day, his bent figure slowly leading the small flock up into the hills or down into the valley below the village. Ayla possessively looked after milking the ewes so Ethan was free to devote his time to the loom and his evenings were spent in delicate carving.

The local carpenter helped and advised him. Sometimes Ethan would disappear for hours at a time and return loaded down with all shapes and sizes of beams and wooden rods.

Judith puffed her way home from the market one day to find the loom set up. She circled it, touching the beams and the heddels that Ethan had carved with such love and care. "I can make even more robes and blankets to sell in the market." She envisioned the future, weaving clothing for their family and a profitable business besides. There was a commotion at the door and Ethan's parents entered. With a grandchild on the way, Ayla was a changed woman.

"We came to see the new loom. Ahhh! Much easier on the back!"

"Why don't you spend the afternoons here, Mother?" Ethan suggested. "You used to spin when you were young. Maybe you want to start again."

"Look at the wool for the baby's shawl." Judith showed Ayla some she had spun as fine as a spider's web. "I'm going to start on it right away. You can keep me company." Ethan's mother picked up some raw wool and began to fluff it with her fingers, preparing a rogleg of wool that would later be spun out with the spindle. Old habits quickly resurfaced.

"You have warped a loom before, yes? You want I should send Nina over to teach you? For years she has helped her mother weave."

"Nina would do that for me?"

"If I tell to come, she'll come!" When she left later, she stated that she would send Nina over the next day.

"Jacob told me Ethan had finished your loom," Hannah announced as she too appeared later that same day. "Look what he sent for you." She handed Judith a great number of the disks she thought had been Jacob's errors. "He only asks that you make a robe for him in return."

Judith took the disks, hoping Nina would know how to use them.

"I will make him a very nice robe," Judith assured her, "but first I will make one for my baby." The two friends chatted as they examined the loom, talking about all the things Judith would make in the years ahead.

Nina came the next day as soon as Ethan and his father had left. Judith could see similar family traits in Nina and Ethan.

"I will tell you how to do it, but I will not do it for you," Nina informed Judith.

"That way you will learn faster. First, we must wind the yarn around two stakes set at a proper distance in the floor. We will make a small blanket first."

Judith followed Nina's instructions carefully, making the length of yarn exact. Nina showed her how to insert a rod at each end of the wound wool, lift the yarn off the stakes and carry it to the loom, fastening one end to the cross beam.

"This is a lengthy job," Nina stated as she explained how to weave the warp threads through the heddles. "Each one must go through an opposite heddle. This is what makes the shed, or tunnel for the shuttle to go through." Following Nina's instructions, Judith wove each thread through an opposite heddle and tied a pottery disk on the end to pull the thread taut. Twice Judith had to undo some of her work because the threads were twisted, but Nina never lost patience.

Judith heaved a sigh of relief when the entire loom was prepared. She was finally ready to weave.

"See how the heddles lift every other length of yarn when you push on the foot pedal," Nina moved the heddles up and down. With each movement of the foot pedal, half the heddles would rise, making a triangular tunnel through which the shuttle could zip.

Raising the warp threads and opening the shed, as the tunnel was called, Nina deftly slid the shuttle through to the other side and packed the horizontal weft thread firmly in place using the beater bar. Then she raised the opposite heddles and slid the shuttle back through the new tunnel. "Now it's your turn."

Judith sat awkwardly at the loom. She slowly raised the heddles, slid the shuttle through, and got it all tangled up in the strings. With Nina's help, Judith untangled the shuttle.

Over and over Nina showed Judith what to do, guiding Judith in how a certain twist of the wrist could shoot the shuttle all the way through the shed. Over and over the yarn went from side to side. Judith quickly caught on to how to pack the weft thread with the beater bar.

"Go slowly. You will soon learn," Nina reassured Judith as she prepared to return home.

Judith watched her retreating figure and realized that Nina was the most gracious person she had ever met, a wonderful person to have for a cousin.

Judith was a fast learner and during the remainder of her pregnancy she made some of her finest blankets, rivaled in softness only by the new silk fabrics being imported from the East for the Roman rulers.

Then after months of eagerly waiting, two long days of dull aches culminated with the crescendo of wrenching pain and screams. The midwife came and Ethan was banned from the house, every scream tearing at his heart.

Chapter 6

"YOUR SON!" The midwife laid the infant in Judith's arms.

"He's perfect. Has Ethan seen him? Bring Ethan in so he can see his son."

Ethan's hair was sticking out every which way. His face looked haunted, and his hands were clutched behind him to hide their shaking. His first glance was at his wife; Her groans of agony still shuddered through him so he was thankful and relieved to see her alive.

"Are you all right?" He rushed to her side and his expression changed to joy when he saw that Judith was holding their new son. "He's so tiny."

"Look at him, Ethan. Isn't he beautiful? He is worth every agonizing moment." She unwrapped the tiny infant and together they marveled at his tiny toes, his perfect ears and the softness of his swarthy skin. The midwife washed the baby and rubbed salt all over him. Then she gave him back to Judith and departed.

The baby's healthy yell when he was hungry or wet amused them. His voracious appetite amazed them. Judith kept him swaddled in soft linen and covered with a fine wool blanket.

Noam and Ayla rushed over when word got to them that Judith had delivered a son. "Bubeleh," Ayla cooed to the baby, blessing him by calling him a future grandparent. "His name must have meaning," Ethan's mother advised them. "Jacob is a good name. Or Joshua."

"Yes, we must choose a name that is befitting our first-born," Ethan agreed, "a name that will be respectable when he becomes a man." They listened to all the suggestions that came from friends and family but they took the time they needed to choose his name with care. In the end their choice surprised everyone.

When the baby was eight days old, on the appointed day of his *Brit Milah,* Ethan didn't sleep, watching and protecting their son from evil, he studied as he kept vigil on this important night.

Judith was up early making preparations for the family and friends that would celebrate with them. She positioned a chair for Elijah, the Angel of the Covenant, the Children's Protector. By ones and twos their family and friends assembled and both Ethan and Judith took delight in all the fussing and cooing as they showed off their firstborn son.

Jacob and Hannah openly showed their delight in Judith's new son. Years earlier Ethan and Judith had attended Joatham's *Brit Milah* and now they reveled in this wonderful event. "A long life to you," was their blessing.

"It is time to light the candles." Judith was reverently performing that task when the *mohal* arrived, dressed in white, and went with the men into the second room. Ethan took the baby and left Judith with the women.

Hannah placed her arm around her friend, knowing the feelings of pride that accompanied this event and yet, the bit of anguish that filled a mother's heart.

In the other room, with mixed feelings, Ethan laid the baby in the arms of the *mohal*. He, in turn, laid him in the arms of their friend, Jacob, whom they had chosen to be the *sandak*, or godfather.

"Praised be Thou, O Lord our God, King of the Universe, Who hast sanctified us with Thy commandments and commanded us concerning the rite of circumcision," the *mohal*, the village circumciser, chanted, after laying out the tools of his trade. He cut the baby's foreskin, making sure he spilled a drop of blood.

Ethan gritted his teeth as the baby jerked in pain.

Judith's heart wrenched as she heard her infant scream in spite of the honey-soaked cloth Jacob held for him to suck on.

The *mohal* raised his voice louder.

"Praised be Thou, O Lord our God, King of the Universe, Who has sanctified us by Thy commandments, and hast bidden us to make him enter into the covenant of Abraham our father." The chanting continued above the baby's cries. All the men responded in unison, "As he has been introduced into the covenant, so may he be introduced to the study of the Law, to the nuptial canopy, and to good deeds."

They named the baby Jair.

"Aaaaah! The father of Mordecai who helped Esther save our people from destruction." Their choice pleased everyone, even Ethan's mother.

"Yes, Jair means *Enlightens*," Ethan added. "Also a descendent of the tribe of Benjamin. Rachel bore Benjamin right here in Bethlehem. One of the judges of Israel was named Jair too. He had thirty sons who rode on thirty ass colts and they had thirty cities. May our son bring enlightenment to our family and be as fruitful as Jair who judged Israel."

"Come everyone, eat," Ayla called. "Look, fish for fertility, and sweets, symbol of the future." The sumptuous feast was befitting to the occasion.

Judith rocked the fretful baby and dreamed of the future, and friends and family laughed and talked and ate long into the evening.

"So be it!" She murmured into his downy hair, stroking the velvety soft skin on his face. "You are blessed!" Prying open his tiny fist she was in awe at the delicate fingers and miniature fingernails, kissing each one, ten feathery kisses.

"I'm sure we can be forgiven a little bit of pride, yes?" Ethan's face creased with a grin as he held his son after they had bidden farewell to their guests. "I've never seen such a beautiful baby, our innocent son." He pulled the baby close and nuzzled his head, remembering the scream that had issued from the tiny body as the knife did its sanctifying work.

"That's a father speaking," Judith replied, her eyes full of love as she watched the two men in her life. "I know he is special. Our innocent son and he is blessed. He has entered into the covenant of Abraham." Gently she adjusted the robe slightly around the precious bundle, her heart swelling with pride too. The birth of a son had placed her in the ranks of the blessed women of Israel.

"Praise be to God," she breathed under her breath. "I have finally fulfilled the hopes of this family. You, my blessed son, are the next generation."

The small courtyard on top of the house was her favorite place. There the baby nursed at her breast at night, the two of them beneath the stars. Judith cherished this time the most as she sang a lullaby of hope.

"Praise waiteth for thee, O God, in Zion: and unto thee shall the vow be performed: O thou that hearest prayer, unto thee shall all flesh come," Judith sang, running her fingers through Jair's soft, dark curls, so much like his fathers. "May my son become a *chachem,* a wise, learned man." Stars twinkled above. A soft breeze wafted in from the sea. Even the presence of the Roman rulers controlling their land couldn't take this joy from her. "Blessed is the man whom thou choosest and causest to approach unto thee, that he may dwell in thy courts."

"I MUST TAKE Jair to a Levite today to be redeemed," Ethan said as soon as he woke up on the thirty-first day after the baby's birth. "He is our firstborn male."

"I'll get him ready right after we eat," Judith replied. "You have the money, yes?" Later, as she watched Ethan leave with the baby in his arms she smiled at the proud strut in his step. Jehovah had entrusted certain rituals to the father of a male child. This was one of them.

Ethan walked eagerly to the home of the Levite, his infant son nestled in the crook of his arm, a purse of money tied to his belt.

"This, my firstborn son, is the firstborn of his mother," Ethan said as he placed Jair in the arms of the Levite. Pulling the small bag of money from his garment, Ethan continued. "And the Holy One, blessed be He, has given command to redeem him, as it is said: *And those who are to be redeemed, from a month old shalt thou redeem, according to thine estimation, the money of five shekels.*" Ethan placed the money in the Levite's hand.

The Levite returned Jair to his father's arms. "This is instead of that, this is in commutation for that, this is remission of that," the Levite intoned, holding the money over the baby's head. He placed his hands on Jair's head and intoned. "The Lord is thy guardian: The Lord is thy shade upon thy right hand. For length of days, and years of life, and peace shall he add to thee. The Lord shall guard thee from all evil: He shall guard thy soul."

Ethan gently, but proudly, carried his redeemed son home. It was Ethan who coaxed the first smile from the chubby, happy baby. It was Ethan who walked the floor at night, allowing the baby to chew on his roughened knuckle, and who then told the whole village when the first tooth finally poked through.

"Now I have a good purpose for all the wool I haven't combed yet." Using the bulky wool, Judith made a large floor mat for the baby to play on. As he learned to roll over and then to crawl, she added to it, until it covered almost the whole room. Delight shone in her eyes as she watched Ethan play with the baby in the evening, responding to every gurgle, telling him stories from the Torah even at his young age. Her days and nights were devoted to Ethan and Jair. Her dreams had all come true and she praised Jehovah for all of it.

"The robes and blankets, they are taking over our house," Ethan stated the day Jair took his first wobbly step. "We need to sell some of them so we have some room. It would be hard to take the baby to Jerusalem, so maybe I should go alone." He sorted through the mound of blankets and robes Judith had piled neatly behind the door. "These blankets are so soft and woven so well, I'm sure we'll sell them for a good price."

"I almost hate to sell them." Judith ran her hand over the top blanket. "The robes will sell fast. The cold weather is coming and people will be looking for warm robes. Are you sure you want to do this? You'll probably get teased about doing a woman's work."

"Let them tease. I have a good reason to help you with your work. If you pack me some food, I'll leave first thing in the morning. I can set up the stall as soon as I get there and maybe sell everything the next day. I shouldn't be gone more than a couple days."

"This will be the first time I've been away from you, little one." Ethan lifted Jair high into the air. "I'll miss you. You will be good for your mama while I'm gone, yes?" The baby showed off his tiny white teeth in a wide grin and his fingers entangled in his father's curly hair as he came down again, laughing gleefully. Ethan doubled over, holding his son with one arm as he tickled the little tummy to loosen his son's tight grip on his hair. Father and son giggled together, one a miniature replica of the other.

A picture of Ethan as a child suddenly flashed through Judith's mind.

Judith was already mixing the ingredients for barley loaves in her mind when she rolled off her sleeping mat before sunrise the next morning. She quickly followed through with the chore and the mouth-watering scent of fresh bread and the rattle of pots and dishes finally pulled Ethan from his dreams. Jair, curled in a ball, slept in a basket nearby.

Ethan stretched lazily and then, remembering his mission for the day, jumped up quickly. The robes and blankets were tied, well-balanced on the back of the small grey donkey by the time Judith called him to eat. Fresh orange juice sent its tangy scent through the room.

"Delicious!" Ethan mumbled with his mouth full as he heaped pickled tuna on the fresh barley bread and popped a piece of juicy melon into his mouth with the next bite. The salad and olives quickly disappeared along with more bread. It was still early when he left for the city, more fresh bread in his hand and in his bag.

Judith smiled at him. She was always amazed that his delight in food never waned.

"We're going to get plenty of work done while Papa's away," Judith murmured to the baby as she began to work on the wool, pulling the tags, clumped with dirt and manure from the edge of each fleece.

"Oh no, Jair," she gasped as she pulled a dirty bit of wool from the baby's mouth. "That's not to eat," she scolded. She quickly found some bits and pieces of wood to keep him occupied. "Bubbeh will be here soon and then you'll have someone to play with." Ethan's mother had jumped at the chance to keep Judith company each afternoon while Ethan was away. Judith had seen the older woman soften since the arrival of the baby and she now welcomed her company. Washing the fleece was a slow and tedious job, but Judith applied her usual diligence as she scrubbed it clean and then laid it, a bit at a time, in the sun to dry. "Hopefully, most of it will be dried before the cold weather arrives," she whispered softly to herself.

"Are you going to warp the loom and start weaving again?" Ethan's mother asked later as they worked together.

"It would be great to get that done while you're here to help with the baby," Judith replied. "It won't take nearly as long to set up the loom with Jair out of the way. Help me choose the colors and I'll get started." Together the two women agreed on soft gray for the background, red and yellow for the pattern. Then Judith began the long process, fastening one end of the yarn to the cross beam and then, one by one, weaving the warp threads through the heddles, every other one through an opposite heddle. As the women chatted, Judith heard about Ethan's childhood.

For the first time, Ayla quietly shared how she had given birth to one baby after another, only to have them die within weeks. No one could explain why only Ethan lived.

Judith was astonished. No wonder the woman doted on Ethan. So many questions were answered that day. There was a new meaning to the joy in Ayla's eyes as Judith left grandmother and baby alone while she went for water.

Chapter 7

"YOU MISS YOUR papa, yes?" Judith asked Jair at bedtime. "I think he's missing you too. It's the first time he's been away from you. Mama has a secret. Since the day we married, he has not left me. I miss him too." The days sped by, but the nights seemed unusually long.

"Listen! Papa is coming," Judith hurried to the door with her son on her hip as she heard Ethan approaching on the third day. Jair squealed at the sight of his father and with both arms extended, almost leapt out of his mother's arms.

Ethan strode up to the house and snatched the child from Judith's precarious grip. So contented was Jair in his father's arms, that whenever Ethan tried to set him down on the floor he would curl up his legs and refuse to stand. Laughingly, Ethan carried him. Ethan couldn't take his eyes off his son.

"So, are you glad to see me too?" Judith finally asked with a grin. She was rewarded with a quick kiss and a hug before Ethan turned his attention back to playing with the baby. Slowly the evening descended. Judith worked at the loom and shared all the local gossip with her husband, filling him in on the past few days. Shadows danced on the walls as the shuttle whizzed back and forth on the loom and they talked late into the night.

"I heard an odd bit of news," Ethan finally stated after he had heard all of Judith's news. Jair had fallen asleep in his father's arms.

Judith paused in her weaving. Ethan always brought interesting news home from the city. "What?" She waited eagerly for Ethan to continue.

"There were some Eastern Magi in Jerusalem awhile ago looking for a new King of the Jews." There was a quiet pause as Ethan cuddled the sleeping baby and let Judith mull over that bit of news.

"To have our own king again would be wonderful, yes? Is it possible?" Judith asked. "How would Magi from the east know?" Judith looked over her pattern, searching for any flaw that would mar the weaving. She looked to Ethan for more information.

"They were astrologers and had seen a new star that indicated a Jewish king had been born. They were probably Chaldaeans. Remember the story of Daniel and how he became ruler over some of the land where he was a captive? That's the same area. I'm sure they would have learned a lot about our nation while our people were captive there."

"Isn't that the area where Shem, son of Noah settled after the flood? I remember hearing that during the reading of the Torah."

"Yes, and Jehovah called Father Abraham out of Ur of the Chaldaeas too. Our people seem to be joined in the past with that area."

"Tell me more." Judith was enthralled.

"People are saying they asked all around where the *king of the Jews* had been born. Herod was upset, of course. He was also very surprised when he called the chief priests and scribes and discovered that they knew from the Scriptures that the baby was born in Bethlehem."

"What nonsense! I know for a fact that not one family in Bethlehem is related to royalty." Judith stated.

"Well, Herod sent the Magi here to Bethlehem anyway. He was livid when he discovered they had gone directly home without telling him what they found. You know what Herod is like when he's furious. By the time Herod realized they had gone they were probably half way home."

"So Herod would be so foolish to believe them? We don't have a king now, so how could a new king be born? He would have to be born to a king, wouldn't he?"

"Everyone is talking about it," Ethan added, without answering her question. "Some of the people are excited but most are scared. Herod will never allow anyone to displace him as king. He is still sending out people to find that baby."

"It would be wonderful, yes? To have our own king. It all sounds very strange. I would have loved to have seen Magi if they did come here to Bethlehem. What do you think they were like? Why do you think they came?"

"The Persian Empire right now is ruled almost entirely by Magi, brilliant people who seem to know everything that happens in the world. They are the absolute kingmakers in the Persian Empire. No one is allowed to become a king without their approval. I can't imagine them coming all that way unless they were certain of it. I'm curious but perhaps we'll never know more than that."

Jair, asleep in his father's arms, had curled up in a warm little ball. Ethan finally laid him in his bed with a soft kiss on his cheek. The baby sighed and snuggled down on the cot while Ethan and Judith together blew out the lamp. Judith was thrilled to be back in her husband's arms again.

Rumors continued to filter through from Jerusalem as the weeks passed, and the more they talked about it the more people remembered. Some people thought they had seen Magi in town months ago but no one could remember who they came to see or where they went. The memories of that time were of crowds of people coming to Bethlehem to register. Some stayed for days, weeks, months, but none of them appeared to be of royal descent.

People traveling to Egypt from the northern part of Rome were a common sight and still the caravansary at the edge of the town was always busy. Very few travelers ever came right into the town but their gossip did. The stories flew around Bethlehem, grew and spread like a fire in the small village. And as time passed, Herod was becoming more and more obsessed with the thought of a Jewish king.

Noam, a shepherd himself, remembered fellow shepherds who had talked about seeing a baby but no one knew whom the couple was or where they went. As far as they could recollect, this took place even before the mention of the Magi. They had also seen bright lights and visions in the sky. The opinion of most was that the shepherds had seen things out in the fields through wine-reddened eyes.

ETHAN WAS HAVING a nightmare. People were shouting.

"Ethan! Wake up!" Judith shook him. "Something awful is happening." It couldn't be a nightmare. Judith was hearing it too. The high pitched keening of women filled the night

"Hide the baby!" The door of their house burst open and Ethan's mother ran in, screaming. Slamming the door shut she threw all her body weight against it to hold it shut. Her hair was loose and tangled. Her whole body was shaking. She screamed again as she gasped for breath. "Quick! Hide the baby! The Roman soldiers are in town killing babies."

"What's the matter with you?" Ethan put his hands on his mother's shoulders to move her away from the door. "Why are you talking nonsense?"

"They have the census list," she screamed. "They know where every baby is." She pushed at Ethan, trying to turn him around and make him move. Then, in despair, she covered her face with her hands and sank to the floor, wailing, still leaning against the door. Great racking sobs ripped through her aged body. "Too late! Too late!" She sobbed. The sounds of a mob running and shouting in the street grew closer.

"Judith, take Jair and hide in the olive grove," Ethan stated. He had hardly finished the sentence when the house shuddered. A huge weight hit the door with a dull thud, over and over.

In the second room, Judith plucked Jair out of his cot and ran to the inner courtyard. There was no way out except to go back through the other room or scale the wall. Clutching the baby to her breast, she crouched in a corner, hiding under the fleeces, behind a row of crocks.

Even with both Ethan and his mother braced against the door it was forced open, one thunderous blow at a time, sliding Ayla's prostrate body along the floor inch by inch.

"Where did you hide the baby?"

Three uniformed men pushed their way from one room to another, upsetting anything that could hide an infant. Ethan tried to block their way at every turn. As they entered the courtyard, Ethan pushed himself between the men and the corner where his wife and baby crouched, prepared to fend off the intruders and protect his loved ones with his life if need be.

His mother, impelled out of her anguish by overwhelming rage, came diving at the men from behind, slashing at them with a broom. The scuffle lasted only a few seconds before they smashed Ethan against the wall. Systematically they went around the courtyard, poking into bundles, upending everything and finally, scattering the pile of fleeces.

Chapter 8

"NOOOOO!" JUDITH SCREAMED as they tore the baby from her arms before she could even turn away to protect him. Jair screamed in terror as his arms reached toward his mother. One of the soldiers drove his sword through the tiny body. Jair jerked and was silent. Blood sprayed the walls.

"If this was the new king, he's dead now," the man yelled and dropped the baby on the floor. His sword left a trail of dripping blood as they ran out the door.

A scream echoed from wall to wall. Judith sank to the floor beside her son, gently picked him up and pressed him against her breast, rocking back and forth, back and forth, as Ethan wrapped his arms around both of them. The screaming went on and on until Judith realized she was the one screaming. Blood pooled on the floor, stained their hands, and soaked into their clothing. The baby's chubby pink cheeks turned grayish white as life drained away. Judith knew the moment life left him because something within her died with him. Hunched over the baby they wept and screamed and rocked the lifeless body of their son.

Ethan's mother lay in a crumpled heap, wailing in anguish. Time stopped as they huddled there, their screams and cries blending with those of other families in Bethlehem as the scene was repeated in every household that had a baby boy.

"No! No! No!" Judith groaned in denial. Maybe she would wake up and it would be a dream. Reality was much worse than denial.

It fell to Ethan to wash his son's tiny body and anoint it all over with scented oil, the salt of his tears mingling with the sweetness of the perfume. His gentle hands wrapped the little body in long strips of linen made for burial, placing spices in the folds. Then he tore his own clothes in anguish and anger, *Kriyah,* feeling his insides being torn in the same way by the grief he felt. His ripped garments would never be mended, a constant reminder of his grief. It was also Ethan's duty to arrange for the baby's burial.

"Why weren't our sons protected as they were at the Passover?" the people cried to the rabbi. "When will the Lord deliver us from the hands of the Romans as He delivered our people from Egypt?"

Sorrowful howls and wails continued to rend the air at the cemetery. The recitation of the *Kaddish*, meant to bring forth cleansing tears, only partially did its work. The tears flowed freely, but they were not cleansing anyone as family after family buried their infant sons. The entire village mourned.

They lingered at the graveside, reluctant to leave their baby alone with the elements. Finally, Jacob and Hannah turned them and pushed them towards home.

"What home?" Judith spat out as they mentioned the word. "It will never be a home again." On their return from the cemetery, friends and family awaited with a meal of recuperation, meant to sustain them and show them that life must go on. Judith took no pleasure in it. She didn't want life to go on.

It was the first meal in over a year when she had not hovered over Jair and spooned food into his hungry little mouth. Conversation consisted of discussing the event repeatedly. "Come, eat! Tell us every detail."

"I know we need to be ritually cleansed because we touched a dead body but our son was killed and we comforted him as he died." Judith sobbed to Ethan. "I know it's for our protection but it's like we're washing away the last evidence of his life. It hurts so badly!" Their three days of deep grief passed but seemed to last a lifetime. Judith continued to produce milk until the physical pain became almost as unbearable as her inner pain. She couldn't eat. She couldn't sleep.

"How can people go on with life?" She sobbed. "The world should stop! My baby is dead!" Every night she wept in Ethan's arms and it didn't ease her grief to know that in Bethlehem every boy under the age of two had been murdered.

Ethan often disappeared into the hills where he wept, beat his breast, yelled at the sky and prayed prayers he would never allow Judith or his parents to hear. And when he came home, he was calm, a rock for Judith to lean on.

"More than twenty babies were killed in this area," Ethan said as they lay awake holding each other one night. "The rabbi said they killed every baby boy; not one was missed. It was another of Herod's senseless massacres. When will it stop?"

The week of shiv'ah, deep mourning, passed with a constant stream of people coming to grieve with them, each demanding another recounting of the death

Thirty days of lesser mourning crept past but the grief had not lessened for them. They learned to go about their work every day wondering why. They didn't feel like eating, or washing, or combing their hair. Days passed, then weeks and months. Slowly the Jewish period of mourning passed. Reluctantly, outwardly, Ethan and Judith acknowledged God's will.

Purim marked the beginning of spring and celebrated the story of Esther. Judith dutifully made the little apple filled pastry triangles called *Haman's Ears,* and the tears flowed as she remembered how Jair loved chewing on them, poppy seeds sticking to his nose. Everything she did contained memories of her baby.

Ethan immersed himself in work.

"Can I help with the sheep?" Judith finally asked during lambing season when Ethan was leaving the house. "I need something to fill my days." Eagerly, she went with him, hoping for a reprieve from her memories. She was not prepared for the intense feelings that would well up within her and the new torrent of scalding tears that would gush forth when she saw each ewe with her newborn lamb. Loneliness swept over her again.

She cried with the bleating of the ewes whose lambs had died.

Ethan's heart almost broke as he saw her weeping over a dead lamb. There had been tears in his own eyes as he and his father performed the heart-wrenching job of skinning the dead lamb and using the skin to trick a ewe into accepting an orphaned lamb in place of her own. It was the only way to save the life of another lamb.

Judith's heart went out to the ewes being tricked. She couldn't imagine another baby taking Jair's place. "I'm going for a walk," she stated bluntly.

Ethan watched with concern as, head bowed, she trudged up the stony slope, thistles pricking her bare feet at the sides of her sandals. Fields of spring flowers covered the hillside. Every crevice, crack and ledge revealed vegetation, green from the spring rains. Ignoring the new growth, she chose instead to set her gaze over the barren hills on the other side of the valley. Pulling her gown together into a pouch she began gathering dried dung to burn in the hearth.

"Even dung has its uses, but I am absolutely worthless. Of less value than dung. Oh, God, why has this happened? Why did you take my baby?"

Mother birds feeding their young caused raw wounds to rip open. Springtime screamed new life at her, but she felt only death. The spring rains washed away the dust outside but did nothing to cleanse within.

Gradually the eleven months, meant to bring healing, passed. The tears dried on the outside but continued to fall within her heart. There was no healing. Like the blood stains still on the wall, grief wouldn't go away. Ethan had finally put another layer of mud and straw over the area but the stains were still there, hidden, like her inner pain.

Automatically, Judith prepared everything they would need for the entire Sabbath the day before so there would be no cooking done on their holy day. She still lit the Sabbath candles exactly seventeen minutes before sundown, repeating the prayers and blessings that went with the ceremony. She would not allow even her sorrow to stand in the way of her duties to her faith. Ethan came home for the evening meal after joining the men at the synagogue. Two loaves of bread, symbol of God's bounty, had their special place on the table. Often Noam, Ayla and Nina came to eat with them. Judith didn't feel quite so lonely when they were there. Ethan passed the glass of wine, which each of them sipped, and each took a small piece of the bread. Judith tried to concentrate on God's bounty as each Sabbath came and went. She tried hard.

"Jair would be two today," Judith told herself when his birthday came. The next year it was "Jair would be three today." Mothers of other murdered infants bore children to fill their empty arms. Hannah gave birth to another son and they named him Oshea but Judith's arms remained empty, her womb unproductive.

"Have mercy on me, O God," she prayed when she went to the temple in Jerusalem. "Blot out my transgressions. Cleanse me from my sin. I'll do anything you ask of me, only give me another son." Like Hannah, she wept before the Lord. "There must be sin in my life or else why would the Lord do this to me?" She prayed and pled, made deals and promises.

She watched in envy as parents escorted their sons to school at *bet hasefer*, the 'house of the book'. The synagogue, where the entire village gathered each Sabbath to hear a portion of the Torah read, also served as the school. It was the center of the community. Judith felt lonelier there than at any other place in the village. Everyone else was busy with their families. The year Jair would have been old enough to start school, the whole village was aware there was not one boy to attend.

"I won't go to bet hasefer." she stated one day when the community was gathering for a family event. "I can't stand being with all those families."

"I think Hannah wants you there," Ethan coaxed.

"Hannah has her own family to look after," Judith replied sadly. "She won't miss me. Anyway, she feels guilty when she sees me."

"Guilty? Why should Hannah feel guilty?" Ethan asked in surprise.

"Because she has her children and I have none. She doesn't know what to say to me. If she talks about her children she feels bad and if she avoids talking about them she feels worse. Other women scorn me and Hannah thinks she betrays them if she befriends me."

With a heavy heart Ethan went to bet hasefer without her.

"Maybe if we pray hard enough Jehovah will hear us and give us another child," Judith suggested. She knew that God could answer their prayers for another baby but as each year passed that hope dwindled. They kept The Law, so that couldn't be the problem. They never missed going to the synagogue on the Sabbath.

The entire Torah was read through each year, reading a portion each Sabbath. The Sabbath Ethan took his turn the account of Abraham offering his son, Isaac, as a sacrifice was given him to read.

"If Jehovah had asked me to give my son, like Abraham, I would have done it willingly," Ethan said vehemently as they walked home later. "I just can't stand the fact that Herod, that diabolical ruler, killed him. If only it had been for Jehovah."

"ETHAN SHOULD DIVORCE you and marry a young wife to give him sons!" The first time Judith heard her mother-in-law utter these words she was shocked. They had been alone and the older woman had gone away with a smug expression. She had struck a tender spot. A new fear began to grow in Judith. Was she being unfair to Ethan?

The one reprieve from the routine of daily life was their market trips to Jerusalem with their donkey almost buried under a load of Judith's woven robes and blankets, ready to sell at the market.

"Come and celebrate Seder with us," Hannah begged, referring to the ceremonial meal on the first night of Passover. "Maybe it will be easier this year." Passover was especially hard for Judith and Ethan even though years had passed and the ache within had become a dull pain. Judith looked for an excuse not to go, but Ethan's parents went to be with Nina's mother and father. Even being with Hannah's family would be better than being alone.

Judith paced from room to room at home that day. She knew that Hannah would spend the entire day searching her house for any sign of leaven. She would move everything; cleanse every inch of the dwelling. Judith wondered if she should be there to help. But Tirzah was old enough now to help her mother.

"Come, help me prepare the food," Hannah begged.

Judith had no excuse to give. The children, even young Oshea were quiet and subdued, sensing how sacred this ritual was. Judith helped Hannah prepare the food as Tirzah set the table according to their traditions. Then Judith placed the three-layered matzah cakes representing the Priest, the Levite and the Israelite on a plate. Hannah prepared the bitter herb salad on another plate, and the charoseth sauce, made of ground nuts, fruits and wine, on a third. The shank bone of lamb had a special place.

A mixture of feelings washed over Judith as she and Ethan joined Hannah, Jacob and their children around the table bathed in the glow of lantern light.

"Blessed art Thou, Eternal our God, Ruler of the universe, Creator of the fruit of the vine," Jacob intoned.

"Blessed art Thou, Eternal our God, Ruler of the universe, Creator of light and fire." Jacob washed his hands and then he dipped parsley into salt water and passed it to everyone.

"Blessed art Thou, Eternal our God, Ruler of the universe, Creator of the fruit of the earth," he stated and they ate the bitter herbs.

Jacob broke the middle matzah in half, wrapped one half in a cloth and set it aside. This was afikomin and would be the last thing eaten.

"Why is this night different to all other nights?" Oshea asked the first of four questions after he had read a special passage from the Passover Book, the *Hagadah*.

Judith bowed her head in sorrow. This honor by tradition went to the youngest son and she remembered how she had once dreamed of the day when their son would take his turn. Would she ever enjoy the meal again, she wondered?

Jacob, wearing his hat and coat, carrying a satchel, answered Oshea's question by enthusiastically telling the story of the exodus from Egypt. His hands flew as he illustrated how the people had gathered their belonging and fled. He explained, too, how they left so fast they hadn't had time to bake bread with yeast.

"These three drops of wine remind us of the blood, the fire and the pillar of smoke during the deliverance." Jacob spilled three drops of wine. "These drops of wine remind us of the ten plagues." Jacob dripped wine on the table as he recited each of the ten plagues.

Judith watched Jacob's youngest son silently mouth the words along with his father. Someday he will be teaching these truths to his own son, she thought.

"The lamb, the Passover offering, reminds us that He smote the Egyptians and spared our houses. This matzah is eaten because there was not time for the dough to become leavened. These bitter herbs remind us of the bitter life of slavery in Egypt," Jacob explained to the children as he had every year of their lives. Everyone joined in the chanting of psalms and hymns and then joined together in eating the festival meal.

An extra cup of wine was poured for Elijah, who had never died. Someday he would come, maybe this night, indicating the final redemption of Israel.

"Open the door!" Jacob told his son. Oshea ran to fling the door open in case Elijah, *the children's protector,* had arrived.

Judith and Ethan enjoyed the celebration with their friends in spite of the emptiness within. These growing children were far removed from the infant son that still lingered in their memories.

"It's not right. We should have a son to ask the questions," Judith complained later when they walked home. "Why did Herod do this to us? Why didn't Jehovah deliver us? That's what he did in Egypt at the first Passover. What's the use in celebrating deliverance in Egypt when Jehovah refused to save our babies in Bethlehem? What kind of life is this, living under the bondage of the Romans? I hate them!"

Ethan had no answer for her.

The year Jair and his peers would have turned thirteen was another sad year for the village. There was not one thirteen-year-old boy in all of Bethlehem to celebrate his Bar mitzvah and read the traditional chant in the synagogue.

"This is the day our son would have become a man." Ethan's voice was flat and toneless. "His vote would have counted. There are no more events for us to mark now."

A wrenching pain gripped Judith as she saw the anguished look on his face. A few months later, pain of another kind began for Judith. Genuine physical pain appeared and with it a search for healing from the physicians.

"They all tell me the same thing over and over again," Judith replied in response to Ethan's question about her health. "I'm so tired of hearing it and I think I'll scream if I see another leech or bleeding cup."

Again Ethan escaped to the hills where he could weep and pray, fall prostrate on the ground, and then rise up to be strong for Judith.

Chapter 9

"I KNOW GRINDING the grain is painful. Does your weaving bother you, too?"

"Only a little. It's worth the pain to keep busy."

"You're wearing yourself out with weaving."

"That's good. I want to go to bed exhausted at night. Then maybe I can sleep." The sleepless nights were just a vacuum filled with memories, even after all these years.

Love filled Ethan's eyes. His love for Judith never wavered in spite of hints from his mother that he should find another wife so he could have a son again. Judith lived a life scorned by the villagers because her womb was empty. He would not add pain upon pain but he knew his love didn't fill her empty arms. They questioned Jehovah constantly but their questions went unanswered.

"For what reason I can't bear a child? Have we sinned and don't remember?"

"We've beseeched the Lord over and over," Ethan reminded her. "What more can we do?"

Judith searched for something meaningful to do apart from making and selling garments and robes. Then another thought occurred to her: she had no daughter to teach this wonderful craft of weaving. One day Hannah and Tirzah came to visit. As Judith showed them the robes she had finished she suddenly became aware of the interest in Tirzah's eyes. That image remained in Judith's mind until one day she went to visit Hannah.

"Did Tirzah enjoy her visit to my house the other day?" Judith asked as she joined Hannah in stacking pottery on the shelves.

"She talked of nothing else for days. I've never seen her so excited."

"Hannah. You know I have no daughter to teach. If Tirzah wishes I would like to teach her to weave. Maybe some day my loom will be hers."

"Oh, Judith!" Hannah wrapped her arms around her friend. "Some day you will have another child."

"I keep asking Jehovah to bless us again."

"Do you want to ask Tirzah? Let's go into the house and see what she thinks."

Tirzah was ecstatic. Her dark eyes sparkled with joy and she was ready to start at once."

"I have a robe almost finished. Come tomorrow and see how the loom works, yes?" Judith left with a smile on her face as she looked back and saw Tirzah dancing around the room. That night she sorted through the wool, choosing some she thought Tirzah could start with. Judith was filled with an interesting mixture of feelings. Sorrow that it was not her own daughter she would teach to weave, but excitement at the prospect of such a willing student.

The next day Tirzah arrived at Judith's door. Judith finished her own project and together they threaded the loom. Tirzah had a passion, to create soft, lovely blankets for newborn babies. It took only a couple days for Judith to realize she was a quick learner. Before long every mother giving birth looked forward to receiving a piece of her amazing work.

Years passed and Judith's figure filled out with age. Joatham married but continued to work with his father with the pottery. Judith was amazed at the sorrow she felt when Hannah informed her that a young man from a nearby village had asked for Tirzah's hand in marriage. This young girl had brought light into her life for the past few years. Judith began to feel a sense of panic. She had never totally given up hope but now her childbearing years would soon be over. Then one day a glimmer of hope arrived.

"Ethan! Everyone is talking about the prophet preaching by the River Jordan. You've heard news, yes?"

"Only that they call him John the baptizer, because he's baptizing people in the river. He's a strange fellow, living in seclusion and preaching repentance."

"Can we go and hear him? Perhaps if we submit to this baptism of repentance Jehovah will hear our pleas. I will soon be past my childbearing years and there will be no more hope. Maybe we are childless because we have sinned."

Ethan's brow wrinkled in doubt. "I don't know what we will be repenting of. We can go and see. Perhaps Jehovah will reveal something to us while we're there. I'll listen for news of where this baptizer is.

Judith waited eagerly. Surely sometime soon he would be baptizing in the south portion of the Jordan River. Finally, word came that he was nearby. Judith quickly filled a woven bag with food and whatever else she thought they might need.

Their journey was a steady downhill trip from Bethlehem to the Jordan River. The dry rocky ground gradually gave way to lush grass and shady trees along the river valley. They were not alone on the way. It seemed as if everyone in Jerusalem had come out to hear this man. Crowds lined the banks of the river where the baptisms were taking place. Slowly, bit by bit they were able to shoulder their way through the crowd until they had a clear view. Sunlight glittered on the water while fluffy white clouds floated overhead.

Judith, ever mindful of the varieties of weaving, immediately noticed that the prophet wore sackcloth, a garment signifying penitence, woven of coarse camel hair. A plain leather girdle encompassed his waist.

"Prepare ye the way of the Lord," the preacher said loudly and with authority. "Make straight paths for him. I indeed baptize you with water unto repentance but there cometh one who will baptize you with the Holy Spirit."

Judith glanced around to see what reaction his words were having on the people. Rich and poor of all ages listened eagerly to his words. Judith could pick out some whose wet heads indicated that they had already taken part in this baptism of repentance; their faces glowed with happiness.

When a man entered the water to be baptized, Judith and Ethan watched with interest. Rising up again with water streaming down his face, they could see joy fill his whole being.

"There must be something to this," Ethan whispered. "Look at the expression on his face. I'm glad we came." One by one, people entered the water to be baptized and all the time, this man, John, preached repentance. Finally they could resist no longer. Together they entered the waters of baptism, repenting of any hidden sin there might be in them.

"Oh, Lord, is it the sin of pride?" Judith cried. "I'm sorry we were so proud of our son. I repent of that sin. Cleanse me from secret sin too."

A steady procession of people followed them, all repenting of their own secret sins.

Judith was drying her long dark hair in the sun when a murmur rose from the crowd. While he was still in the water, a dove flew down and sat on a man John had just baptized.

"What a strange thing," Judith thought as the dove sat there. No one made a move to chase the bird away, and it didn't seem in a hurry to leave. People nearby told them the man was John's cousin.

The weather was mild. Ethan and Judith decided to join others who were spending the night sleeping under the stars, with light robes for covers.

"It's been a long time since I have felt so contented," Judith murmured just before she fell asleep. The next morning they nibbled on bread and cheese left from their trip.

"Behold the Lamb of God which taketh away the sins of the world," the baptizer called out as he greeted his cousin again. Heads turned at the loud, forceful cry. Judith and Ethan focused their attention on the pair and watched.

"The one who sent me to baptize told me, '*The man on whom you see the Spirit come down and remain is he who will baptize with the Holy Spirit,*'" John told the assembled crowd. "I saw the Spirit come down from heaven as a dove and remain on him." A murmur went through the crowd again. The story enthralled them.

"I saw that dove," Judith whispered. "What did John mean?"

"I don't know. It is not a doctrine I have ever heard before." They began the return trip home deep in thought but with light hearts.

"What a special time that was," Judith declared. "I'm glad we went. John is an interesting person, yes? His robe was of camel hair. I didn't understand everything he was saying though, did you?"

"I'll have to think about what he said," Ethan replied. "Maybe I'll understand it after I've thought it over." Sunshine warmed them as their route wound through the Jordan Valley, and then climbed the steep, rock-strewn hills to Bethlehem.

Judith worked through her days with a happy glow. Perhaps Jehovah had cleansed some secret sin from their lives during their baptism. She hoped and prayed she would be with child. But surely, if she had been forgiven the pain would be gone, wouldn't it? She pondered often over John the Baptizer, and the austere life he lived.

"I refuse to give in to my pain," she muttered to herself. "I will not admit defeat and ask for help with my work, either."

The bending and sitting as she prepared the wool for spinning continued to cause excruciating pain.

"Lord, cleanse me from secret sin," she said over and over to herself as she pulled the dirty edges, or 'skirtings' off the fleece and her hands became raw and sore as she picked out the thistles and burrs. "All my life I've been taught that you bless those who do good and curse those who don't. What have I done to deserve this pain?"

"I wonder if I should use these skirtings to make cushions or to refill our sleeping mats," Judith asked aloud so Ethan could hear her.

"My mat is still soft enough," Ethan replied from where he sat braiding a new lead rope for the donkey.

Judith decided to finish some cushions she had started weeks earlier. Sewing woven squares together, she used the skirtings as stuffing and soon had several plump floor cushions.

Her slender fingers teased the rest of the wool, pulling it apart until it was light and almost free of tangles.

Some she combed until it was smooth and fluffy, and rolled it into a soft tube or rolag. The pile of rolags, ready and waiting for spinning, continued to grow. Some wool she didn't comb but set aside to spin directly from the fleece for heavier garments and floor mats.

"Oh, how I've failed you, Ethan," Judith whispered as she prepared to attach the wool from her distaff to the spindle. "I had such hopes that I'd be making garments for our children and grandchildren." She spoke softly to herself so Ethan wouldn't hear her lament.

The spindle's wooden rod and the whorl on the bottom were worn smooth from years of use. Attaching a length of wool to the spindle, Judith wrapped it around the bottom knob. With a quick twist of her finger she fastened it with a half hitch to the notch at the top. Moistening her fingers, she pulled some of the fibers from the rolag on her distaff and twisted them into the tail of wool on the spindle.

"Remember when you made this spindle for me, Ethan?" With a flick of her left hand she sent it spinning while her right hand controlled the amount of wool being added. The spinning rod lowered to the floor as the thread grew longer. When it touched the floor Judith wrapped the newly-spun wool up and down the spindle in a criss-cross pattern, and attached it around the knob and up to the notch again.

"I made it the first year we were married." Ethan never tired of watching her spin. There was a kind of hypnotic sequence as the spindle spun and lowered, lifted, spun and lowered. "You could probably do that with your eyes closed." He marveled at how the pile of rolags slowly dwindled and the skeins of spun yarn piled up. Judith liked to have a good supply of wool spun before she began weaving.

"Tears, Judith? The job is so boring it has reduced you to tears?"

"I was remembering the fine soft wool I spun before Jair was born and the lovely robe I gave to Anna that year for her new baby girl. Remember that little robe Jair clung to when he went to sleep? Do you think the memories will ever get any easier?" Ethan didn't answer and Judith continued to work.

Making belts had become painful work for her too, as she sat on the floor, weaving in the old-fashioned way. She waited until Ethan left the house before she fastened the wool on the stakes in the floor. She determined that Ethan would not see her tears and she refused to slow down.

Chapter 10

JUDITH WAS IN a good mood as they walked to their synagogue on *Simhat Torah,* a few weeks later. This was a day of joy and celebration when the reading of the Torah would be completed and immediately begun again.

"Hannah!" Judith saw her friend and called to her. "Come, sit with me." They were filled with anticipation by the time the priest took the meter-high scroll out of its ornate cupboard. In traditional chant the end of Deuteronomy was read, immediately followed by the reading of the beginning of Genesis.

Everyone danced and sang and tambourines added a beat as the scroll was carried out of the synagogue, into the streets. They paraded their joy in the circle of unity, with no beginning and no end of the Holy Law. Judith rejoiced with the rest of the villagers. Perhaps this year would be different. Her feet beat a rhythm on the hard packed earth where generations before her had danced on *Simhat Torah.* Perhaps this would be a year of joy for her and Ethan also.

Even at the end of the day, when they were home alone, their celebrating continued.

Again Judith was disappointed. Totally dejected, she took the discouraging walk to the purification baths. The physical pain continued to worsen. She hid in her house day after day, immersed in her work. She kept a close watch on the women coming and going from the well, often glancing out the door to see if any of the women still lingered on their way home. When the way was clear, she gathered her bucket and water jar.

"I guess it's safe to go now. I'll avoid the looks of pity and scorn for one more day."

Later in the day she balanced a basket of laundry on her head and headed for the stream. No one else was in sight as she washed the clothes. Bend and dip. She gasped as pain shot through her. Ignoring it, she wet the garments, rubbed her homemade lye soap into the cloth and scrubbed them on the rocks.

"Time was when I could work up quite a lather," she spoke out loud to herself. "Now I'm doing well if I can even get the clothes washed." She loaded her wet laundry into the basket. Another pain gripped her as she tried to hoist the burden onto her head. Holding the basket in front of her, hardly daring to breathe, she made her way home. Sweat was dripping down her neck by the time she got the clothes hung out to dry in the covered section of the courtyard. Both washing and hanging the clothes were agonizing jobs for her.

There was no way she could escape the rest of the women when the yearly olive harvest arrived. Everyone harvested their olives on the day set aside by the village for that purpose. After that day, anyone could help themselves to the fruit remaining on the trees. Spreading the olives in the circular trough of the olive mill Judith reached for a stone.

"I'll help you with that," Ethan startled her as he gently moved her aside and took the stone from her.

Judith gave in with relief, as Ethan bent over the mill and pressed the rock down on the olives. She opened one of the woven fiber bags, ready to put the oily pulp inside. Working together, the job would soon be done and they would have fresh oil for the festival of lights which lay ahead.

"I can't put this through the olive press myself," Judith stated, saddened to think she was not able to do all the things a good Jewish wife would do.

When the olive harvest was over Judith began weaving again, stockpiling blankets and robes to take to Jerusalem as the weather turned colder. They could see white patches of snow on the mountain peaks now and their days were cold and wet. Chilling rains beat against the buildings and they were thankful for heavy woolen garments.

Judith lit the *shamash* from a glowing coal and in turn lit a candle on the first night of the Festival of Lights. This was just the first in a series of events they would take part in during this festival. Each night Judith would light another candle until finally there were eight candles flickering on the *Hanukiyah,* a special candelabrum used only for Hanukkah. She place the *shamash* in the center.

"Our history is full of miracles, yes?" Ethan mused on the last night. "Like this miracle, when one-day's worth of oil lasted eight days," referring to the time in their people's history when the Syrians defiled almost all the oil in Israel. Only one small flask bearing the high priest's seal was left for the temple menorah. Only enough oil for one day, but it lasted for eight days. Judah Maccabee and his victorious army rode into Jerusalem on their eighth day. It was truly a miracle when God delivered them from the Syrians.

"The whole story of the Maccabees and what they did for our people is reason to celebrate," Judith added. "I just wish Jehovah would do a miracle for us again." She leaned into Ethan's hug, knowing he shared the desire that filled her heart.

"It's nice to remember all the history of our people, but I would love to see a miracle myself." Again Judith immersed herself in weaving, but always longing, always expecting a miracle.

Weeks passed as Judith stockpiled new blankets and robes to take to Jerusalem. Ethan planted the grain and the spring rains began. The almonds bloomed, new lambs arrived. The warm gentle rains had brought everything to life again. Then it was Passover time again and the barley harvest had to be completed before they could pack up the robes and blankets to go.

Noam and Ethan worked quickly with their scythes to harvest their small barley crop while Judith readied everything for their trip. At least, being in Jerusalem for Passover meant they didn't have to take part in a Passover meal at home or with Jacob and Hannah's family.

"Does it seem as if the crowds get a little larger every year?" Ethan asked as he and Judith approached Jerusalem. He tugged on the rope, moving their loaded donkey a little faster. They hoped to have all the blankets and robes sold before Passover. "Look at the sun shining on the temple. Isn't it beautiful?"

The city lay in descending terraces, drawing ones eyes to the temple. Judith didn't answer as hatred for the Romans rose up within her. She walked with her head bowed, not even looking up to see the crowds.

"Do you think Herod actually made the Temple more splendid than Solomon's Temple?" Ethan tried to get Judith to respond to him. "You have to give him credit for building it for us and for training the priests themselves as masons so the temple would not be defiled." Still Judith refused look at it.

"Herod knows our Law forbids making graven images," Judith finally replied. "This is our Holy Temple and Herod defiled it." She finally raised her head to look at the place where Herod had put a huge golden statue of an eagle above the main entrance.

"The eagle isn't there anymore, Judith," Ethan brushed his hand down her arm. "Our people tore it down."

"I'm glad they did," Judith spat. Finally, she looked at the building. The temple was an immense limestone structure with marble pillars and golden gates. The huge blocks did reflect the sunshine. "I hate the fact that Herod had anything to do with our Holy Temple." She spat on the ground in distaste as they entered the narrow streets and the temple disappeared from her vision.

"Tiras, my friend," Ethan called as they neared the inn where they always stayed. Tiras, the innkeeper, appeared with open arms, loud shouts and laughter.

"Shalom!" Tiras greeted Ethan with a hug and slaps on the back. "Your place is reserved for you. Always, this place is reserved for you, my friend!" He helped Ethan unload the donkey and set up their stall.

"Tomorrow you will buy up all the best spices, yes?" Tiras grinned at Judith. "Everyone knows all the best spices go back to Bethlehem with you. I will help Ethan while you shop."

The scents of sweating animals and people wafted through the air as Judith shoved her way through the crowds in the market place the next day. Caravans from Egypt were unloading spices and linen as well as numerous other items. She ducked her head just in time to avoid being elbowed by a merchant measuring cloth. Leaning slightly to one side to relieve the pain in her side she moved on, determined to finish her shopping before Ethan finished his work.

The singsong voices of vendors pulled her to the spice stalls where delicious odors filled every painful breath. She selected her purchases with care even while being jostled and pushed. She added cheese to her supplies and falafel from a nearby kiosk. She was enjoying the beautiful day, but the aroma of fresh bread made her realize she had one more stop to make at the Street of Bakers.

"I guess my fifty years are beginning to show," she mused, rubbing the palm of her hand over her aching side. "I'm moving more slowly all the time. The pain is always worse when we travel, but I wonder why it didn't go away after a night's rest as it usually does."

Slowly, she walked through the marketplace where the pungent odors of onion and garlic mixed with the smell of fish. At each stall, heaped high with pomegranates, melons and eggs, hovered a noisy seller, coaxing people to buy.

While adults haggled over prices, voices loud in debate, children played games, running in and out between the stalls.

"Judith!" Hannah called from behind her. "When did you get here?" The women greeted each other with smiles. "I wanted to travel with you but Jacob had to be here early to do some business." Hannah, like Judith, had begun to fill out with age, their once slender arms now softly rounded and the backs of their hands dotted with the soft brown spots of aging.

They lingered and visited near a stall where an assortment of exquisite articles from the East was on display. Judith ran her hand over the silk garments and soon Hannah's hand lay on the silk too.

"This is so fine. Did you know the Romans hate the designs that come from the East so much they unravel all the silk cloth and reweave it?"

Judith peered in astonishment at her friend. "How could anyone pick apart such minute fibers?"

"That's the Romans for you," Hannah replied. "They don't do it themselves. They just pay someone else to do all their tedious work. And probably don't pay a very good wage at that. That's why all these beautiful silk fabrics from the East are too costly for anyone but the wealthy to purchase." Hannah moved away from the stall.

"I have to buy bread," she called as she walked away, "but we'll travel home with you after the Sabbath." Judith took a long, deep breath, tired from carefully hiding her pain.

"Judith! What's wrong?" Ethan grabbed her parcels before she dropped them as she entered their booth. "Sit!"

He dragged his own stool close and eased her down onto it. "Is it your side again?"

"It feels better now," Judith stated. "At least I got all my shopping done. I saw Hannah. They want to travel home with us."

"I know," Ethan replied. "I talked to Jacob too. He has sold almost all his pottery already." His face creased in a wide grin. "There must be a lot of broken pots around. Your pain has been getting worse these past weeks, hasn't it?" Concern replaced the grin on Ethan's face. "I should have done the shopping and left you here at the stall."

"But I love the market. You should see the beautiful things they have brought from the East." Judith eased herself off the stool and took her purchases into the inn passing the young leper boy on the way. His big brown eyes filled with sympathy. He had been listening. Judith hurried past him.

"He should feel so bad for me," she muttered. "He has no fingers or toes and half his face is gone.

Chapter 11

"WHO IS HE to feel sorry for me?" Judith lifted her eyes to heaven and thanked Jehovah that she only had a pain. That she could live with. Leaving her parcels, she returned to the stall.

"Did you hear about the prophet from Nazareth everyone is talking about?" Ethan asked when she joined him. She could hear the excitement in his voice. "He is a teacher and also a healer. Maybe he could help you with your pain."

Judith took over the stall while Ethan went off to sit with the other men and discuss the politics of the day. The news about the prophet rolled around in her mind as Judith sat and allowed her pain to subside. When Ethan returned with even more news about this new teacher who could heal it was difficult for her to even imagine someone, a mere man, healing people. She wrapped herself in her thoughts. With darkness had come a certain quiet in the city, although there were still people milling about the narrow lanes. Hungry people would continue to shop at the food stalls until late into the night.

"We should be able to sell everything else tomorrow in time to go to the temple and change our money before the Passover begins." Ethan was closing the stall for the night. The little pile of rags beside the inn didn't move as they went inside. They knew the young leper boy, curled up there for the night.

The next day Judith sat on a stool sorting their money into two small bags, while Ethan dismantled the stall.

"Ech! What profanity!" She spat out the words as she roughly threw the hated Roman coins into one bag, coinage that bore the images of pagan gods and Roman rulers. Into a second bag she placed the *pure money* that bore no images and could be used for the temple tax or to purchase their sacrifice.

"I wish we didn't have to accept this awful currency in order to sell our goods," Judith complained. She grimaced as she threw in one of the coins identifying Tiberius as the *chief priest* of the Imperial Cult. "What blasphemy!"

"At least we can use it to pay our tax to Rome," Ethan reminded her. "The rest we will just have to take to the money changers to be exchanged for *pure* money." Ethan chose a coin from the pile and walked over to the young leper.

"Unclean! Unclean!" The boy cried in a panicked voice, cringing away as Ethan came near.

Puzzled, not that the boy cried out, but that he recoiled, as if expecting Ethan to touch him, caused Ethan to pause and look closer. The wide frightened eyes followed Ethan's every move as he slowly reached down and placed the coin directly into the boy's bowl.

Ethan had seen people throw coins in the boy's direction and also watched him struggle to pick them up from the ground with his misshapen hands. Somehow, he eventually managed to get them into the bowl.

The crowd hadn't thinned at all. It seemed to grow more dense as Judith and Ethan wound their way past the market halls, the barracks, the Fortress of Antonia and climbed up towards the temple. There seemed to be some excitement ahead but the crowd was so dense they could hardly move. Ethan plowed a path through the crowd for Judith, who followed close behind.

"That must be the prophet." Ethan had to speak right into Judith's ear to be heard above the noise of the crowd. "Maybe we should ask him to heal your side."

Judith looked in the direction Ethan had pointed and got her first glimpse of the man he had talked about so much. Her mouth opened in amazement. Could this man be a prophet and a healer?

"He isn't at all what I expected," Judith thought as she viewed the man dressed plainly in a linen robe and sandals. "I had expected to see a man towering above the heads of the people but he isn't even a tall man." He didn't look like a teacher and he certainly didn't look like any of the physicians she had seen over the years. People crowded around him, asking for help, blocking him from her view most of the time.

"We'll never get his attention in this crowd," Judith shouted. She wondered if she would even have the courage to place herself under this man's influence. Were all these people following him blindly because of what he could do?

Did she even want to be a part of that? Could she actually yield to the unknown without understanding?

The man disappeared so Judith and Ethan moved along with the crowds towards the temple that dominated the north of the city. Herod had doubled the size of the court of the Gentiles, trying to gain acceptance from the people he ruled over.

"We have enough for our temple tax," Ethan stated. "We'll exchange the rest of our money when we come out," he added. "The lines are too long now."

Together they passed through one of the seven entrances that gave access to the temple mount. Crossing the courtyard and ascending a flight of steps, they faced the massive stone wall that enclosed the Temple itself. Nine more gates, decorated in gold and silver, confronted them. Judith paused by the gate called Beautiful leading into the women's court, where she would wait while Ethan went on into the temple.

Ethan pulled his prayer shawl over his head and bound a phylactery onto his forehead. Then seven times he wound a strap around his arm, binding another little box to his forearm. These Tefillin contained Scriptures and all the men who had come to worship wore them in literal obedience, to bind the law upon their arms and upon their foreheads.

Judith glanced furtively at the high tower of the Antonia fortress looming in the background. She tugged at Ethan's sleeve and shivered as she tilted her head in that direction, watching Ethan's eyes follow her gaze.

Garrisoned by Roman troops, the red-garbed soldiers stood guard on the porticoes whenever there was a Jewish feast day, watching the entire temple area in case of a riot. Ethan went into the temple while Judith entered the Women's Court. She never found the waiting tedious. She loved watching the people, looking at their clothing, imagining where they were from. She enjoyed speculating from the fabric and weave of their garments whether a person was wealthy or poor.

The moneychangers, wearing silver half-shekels in their ears, reigned at their wooden tables in an area nearby. A brisk business transpired between them and the people, who of necessity had to change their hated foreign currency into useful coins, needed animals, birds or grain for sacrifice, or had come to make money. Upon Ethan's return Judith joined him and they headed in that direction to change their money. Suddenly people and animals began running in every direction. Goats and lambs bawled, women screamed and men shouted. Judith hid behind Ethan and covered her mouth, half in amazement, partly in glee as she watched.

Moments before, the moneychangers had been lording it over the people. Now the moneychangers, on their hands and knees, tried to retrieve their coins that were bouncing and rolling on the ground. The prophet from Nazareth had abruptly interrupted their business. He strode through the hall, upending tables and freeing animals and birds from their wicker cages. The moneychangers yelled in dismay as they crawled around after their money and tried to grab birds and lambs. Judith laughed with glee as people stealthily picked up coins that rolled beneath their feet.

"How dare you turn my Father's house into a market," the prophet denounced the moneychangers. *"Get out!"*

People scurried out of the way of frightened animals. One man grabbed a lamb and quickly turned away.

Would he have the nerve to present a stolen lamb for a temple sacrifice? Judith wondered. Or would he take it home and eventually bring its offspring to the Lord? Silence gradually fell over the crowd as the prophet strode away and only the angry mutterings of the moneychangers continued.

It was a frightening thing to occur in the place of worship yet Judith found a strange fascination in the scene. How quickly the prophet had changed! He didn't seem so much angry as indignant at the profit being made from worship. Perhaps he hated the foreign currency as much as they did. Ethan stood close to her, an air of protection about him. They lingered in confusion, as most of the crowd drifted away.

"What are we going to do now, Ethan? We have all this foreign money and no way to change it for our tithe."

"We may not be able to change it." After a long pause Ethan added, "Unless the money changers set up somewhere else. They'll have to do it quickly because the Passover will be starting soon. I wonder where Jacob and Hannah are?" They walked out of the temple court and joined others standing in small groups, whispering about what had just happened. Some of the highly respected Scribes and Pharisees were arguing with the moneychangers.

"It's hard to tell whether they want the moneychangers to go in and set up again or stay out," Judith said as they watched the exchange.

"Knowing the Pharisees, they will definitely want them to carry on their business," Ethan replied. "Ah! They're going to set up outside the temple walls." He breathed a sigh of relief.

"Get in line quickly," Judith urged him. "There isn't much time left before the Sabbath begins." By the Law, they could not travel on the Sabbath, so they decided to spend the Sabbath at the inn. Tiras, the innkeeper, had exciting news to relate too. He met them at the door of the inn, bouncing with excitement. "Have you heard about Reuben, our young leper friend?" Ethan and Judith glanced at the place where the lad usually sat.

"He isn't there anymore," Tiras added. "Jesus, that prophet from Nazareth healed him. He's gone home to his family." Judith's mouth dropped open in disbelief. Leprosy healed? What did that mean?

"Tell us more." Ethan pressed the innkeeper to continue his story. "What do you mean, he healed him?"

"Really! His hands were restored, every finger like new. It was the most amazing thing."

Judith listened in disbelief. That prophet really did have supernatural powers. It was almost more than she could comprehend.

"We should have pursued him, Judith. Maybe you could have been healed too." Ethan embraced his wife with a faraway look in his eyes.

They left the city as soon as the Sabbath was over, meeting Jacob and Hannah at the city gate. Together they joined a steady stream of people leaving the city that morning. The trip home to Bethlehem passed quickly, with Ethan and Jacob talking about the prophet. Jacob had heard things that Ethan hadn't but Hannah and Jacob had not seen the excitement at the temple, nor had they heard about young Reuben.

As the couples approached Rachel's tomb, just outside Bethlehem, Judith pretended to shake bits of gravel from her sandals, allowing the others to move ahead of her. Wrapped up in discussion, they didn't notice she had dropped back.

Judith gazed at the round white dome that graced the place where Rachel was buried. The tomb had always fascinated Judith and every time she passed it she thought about Rachel.

"Rachel understands!" Judith murmured to herself. "You know what it's like to be childless, don't you? Jehovah answered your prayers with the birth of Joseph. It's too late for me now, but I know you understand." Rachel had suffered ridicule and scorn throughout her childless years before she gave birth to Joseph. She knew Rachel wasn't there to hear her but Judith gazed at the tomb and thought about her ancestor who had died in childbirth right there in Bethlehem when her second son, Benjamin, was born. Memories tucked deep in Judith's heart surfaced every time she walked this road. Today she wondered which was worse, to live on after your child had died or to die as Rachel had and not see her child grow.

"Judith!" Ethan called, "is your side bothering you?"

"No, I'm just slow." Quickly wiping her tears and shaking her foot to dislodge the invisible stones, she quickened her pace to catch up, trying to ignore the pain in her side and the pain in her heart.

✡ ✡ ✡

"Who is this man you're talking about? Tell me!" Ethan's mother demanded. She always watched for them and hurried over as soon as she saw them return from Jerusalem. She was not one to let any news slip past her. It was her primary pastime to monitor what the entire village talked about and then pass judgment on it.

Chapter 12

"He's a new prophet from Nazareth. He has developed quite a following," Ethan explained. "Some people think he may even be the Messiah." He added that information to the account of what had happened in the temple.

"Ha!" The older woman scoffed at her son. "You know nothing! The Messiah is not coming from Nazareth. And he certainly wouldn't do something like that in the temple."

Judith knew enough to keep quiet when the two of them debated. Ethan was a gentle man like his father, and would counter her barbs with gentle but profound words. She wondered sometimes how such a bitter woman could have born such a wonderful son. But then, Judith thought, the woman has good reason to be bitter, and I, Judith, am the one responsible. What really surprised her was that Ethan and his father managed to avoid the bitterness.

Ethan told his mother stories about the prophet. In spite of her attitude, she wanted to hear every detail. Finally Ethan went to help his father with the sheep and left the women alone to divide up the spices Judith had bought in Jerusalem.

"You got me no cloves?" The older woman got up and grabbed her purchases. "You knew I had no cloves. Psha! You never do anything right?" She swept out the door without even a thank you.

"I am supposed to read your mind?" Judith muttered under her breath as the door closed. "I am supposed to know you need cloves when you don't tell me a thing?" Judith heaved a sigh of relief and began putting her own goods away. There was a time when she would have argued, even been tempted to run after her and scream at her. Years of listening to the woman's grumbling and taking her criticism had taught her to keep her mouth shut. Nothing she did ever satisfied that woman.

Picking up one of the pottery jugs Jacob had made for them she headed for the well for fresh drinking water. At least she could have the evening meal prepared for Ethan when he came home and then maybe have time to prepare the loom for weaving again tomorrow. Thankfully, the narrow streets were relatively empty and there was no one else at the well.

"What is the reason for all this?" She questioned. "I go in circles to make money to spend or pay taxes or buy something new. And why? We have no children to leave it to when we die. Why do I even go on living? When I die only the hired mourners will weep for me. Ethan won't mourn for long. He will be free to get himself a young wife and have another son." The thought fermented in her mind as she prepared their evening meal. They ate in silence.

Finally, like a cork popping out of a fermented skin of grape juice, she exploded.

"I want you to divorce me and find yourself a young wife and have another son." Judith almost spat the words at Ethan. "Your mother would be happy and I would be free of my guilt."

"Judith, I would never do that. I love you. You're my life. I love you more than a thousand sons." He could tell by Judith's expression that it wasn't enough. "Am I not enough for you?" Judith's shoulders drooped and tears rolled down her face. Sobs followed the tears as Ethan gathered her into his arms. It saddened Ethan that she had not answered his question.

THE NEXT TIME they prepared to return to the Holy City it was Rosh Hashanah, Memorial of Blowing, the beginning of another new year.

"Maybe Jacob has a load of pottery to take in to sell and we can walk together," Ethan suggested. Judith abandoned her usual furtive trip to the well and timed her errand to meet Hannah there. Hannah seemed pleased to see her and together they made travel plans.

"Jacob does have a load of pottery to take. They'll meet us on the road in the morning to travel with us," Judith told Ethan later. "They'll be staying with Oshea and his family when we get there," Judith turned towards the hearth to hide a quivering lip.

Ethan moved behind her and pulled her to him, holding her in a close hug. He knew what was going through her mind. It was something they didn't talk about but he understood. Hannah and Jacob had sons and a daughter. They had a daughter-in-law and three healthy grandchildren. Judith and Ethan had each other. It never seemed to be enough for Judith.

On this trip they planned to stay in the city for the whole ten days of the festival. Judith loved the blowing of the *shofar*, the ram's horn. It reminded them of Jehovah's love and mercy when God asked Abraham to sacrifice his only son, Isaac. Judith could quote from memory the Scripture telling the end of the story:

"And Abraham lifted up his eyes and looked, and behold, behind him was a ram, caught in a thicket by his horns: and Abraham went and took the ram and offered it up as a burnt offering instead of his son." The ram's horn had a special meaning to her people because of that.

"What a special person Abraham was, willing to give his only son to Jehovah," she thought. "I would have been so willing to give Jair as a sacrifice to Jehovah. Oh, God, why did he have to die such a senseless death?"

The air was chilly and the road crowded with families headed for Jerusalem. Hannah and Jacob waited for them in the early morning freshness, their robes pulled closely around them. Towering piles of pottery rose from the backs of their dark brown donkeys, obliterating even their long floppy ears.

"You want to sell pottery shards in the city, yes?" Ethan teased his friend. "This load will topple over on the hills of Bethlehem, I think. And then you would be selling pottery shards." Jacob was protective of his pottery and balanced his loads with precision. The whole village joked about Jacob's cumbersome loads.

The men walked ahead, each leading a donkey. Ethan led their only donkey, with the bundles of blankets and robes balanced on either side. This way, if the animals swayed the wrong way and the loads collided, Ethan's soft load would not smash the pottery. Judith and Hannah followed, sharing the chore of leading Jacob's second animal. Judith tried to concentrate on Hannah's chatter as they walked past Rachel's tomb. For thirty years this place had reminded her of the reason behind her empty arms. A shiver rippled across her back as she remembered the screams, the blood and the agony. It was an ingrained habit, this remembering.

"Judith, you are dreaming again?" Hannah asked, poking Judith in the ribs with her elbow.

Judith answered with a little laugh and quickened her step. She had not even shared with Hannah, her best friend, how she felt when she passed Rachel's tomb. Hannah wouldn't have understood.

"Remember the last time we went to Jerusalem?" Judith quickly changed the subject. "That prophet from Nazareth drove all the money changers out of the temple. I wonder if he'll be there again?" Judith, trying to disguise the pain that was just beginning to make itself felt again, saw all three turn their gaze on her.

"I've heard lots of stories about him," Jacob replied over his shoulder. "He has developed quite a reputation as a healer."

"The last story I heard was that he commanded a storm to stop," Ethan stated as the two couples continued to pick their way along the stony path. He paused, drawing out the conclusion of the story, until all three stared at him in anticipation.

"So, you don't know the rest of the story?" Jacob finally asked.

"It stopped! The wind and the waves just stopped. Immediately!"

"You think we should believe that someone spoke and the weather changed? Now that's something I'd have to see to believe," Jacob replied. "Who can control the weather? I wish someone could. Then maybe we could do without this bitter wind." As usual the trip did not seem to take long when they visited along the way. Waving good-bye as their friends turned down a side street, Ethan and Judith went on to the inn.

It brightened their day to notice that the leper boy was not there. Judith thought about how joyful his parents must have been when he arrived home, healed. A son, who had been as good as dead, had been restored to life. Judith had seen his deterioration every time they came to the city. Fingers and toes disappeared bit by bit and his face became more disfigured with the passing of time. Only his eyes, full of sadness, never changed.

Ethan set up their booth before the festival began. A new year was the time when people reflected on their lives and behavior during the past year. On the last day of the feast, Yom Kippur, the Day of Atonement, everything in the city stopped. Judith was never content as she reflected over the year. No matter what she did, she always came up short.

"We should find the prophet, Jesus, while we're in Jerusalem and see if he would heal you," Ethan said. His heart ached for Judith. She carried her sorrow, the stigma of barrenness, and the taunting of his mother.

Ethan's parents were old and his mother had not aged well. Her grief at the death of her only grandchild and having no one to receive the inheritance had festered into a devouring bitterness. There was nothing he could do and Judith's added physical pain was almost too much.

"My childbearing time has taken flight," Judith said bluntly, bringing Ethan back to what he had said about the prophet. "It would be a blessing to you if I died and you could find yourself a young wife."

"Judith! I don't want to hear that again. I love you and want you well."

"Maybe that's been the problem all along," Judith retorted. "Once you told me you loved me more than a thousand sons. Maybe too much you love me! Remember Rachel? Jacob loved her and she was barren, while Leah had one baby after another. And Hannah! Elkanah loved her and she was barren, even though his other wife had lots of children. Maybe that's what's wrong."

"Judith, stop! That's nonsense. No one can love too much. Don't ever think that again."

Judith worked quietly beside Ethan but she didn't stop thinking. Her heart swelled with love for him, but she wanted so much more. This festival was ten days long and people had until the last blowing of the shofer on the tenth day to repent. She searched within for something, anything to repent of that would make a difference.

Judith listened discreetly to the chatter of the crowds for word of where the Galilean might be. Fearful, yet excited, she longed to at least talk to the man. Judith felt a tug on her sleeve. Pulling her thoughts back to the present, she turned and looked into the brown eyes of a young boy holding one of her robes. Something about his eyes looked so familiar.

"You dropped this." He placed the robe in her hands.

"Thank you." She turned and put the robe back on the pile.

"You have no son, no?" The boy said softly. Judith turned swiftly, indignant that he would taunt her like that. One look at his expression told her he had not meant it that way.

"No, I have no son," she replied. "Do you live here in Jerusalem? What's your name?"

"My name is Reuben. I used to beg here beside the inn. I had leprosy, but Jesus healed me." Judith leaned forward and looked into the boys eyes.

"I am to believe that you, such a beautiful boy, are the same one we saw here?" Even as she doubted, she knew she would recognize those eyes anywhere. "How wonderful!" Judith breathed softly. "Ethan! This young man is Reuben, the young leper that used to beg here by the inn. Jesus healed him." Judith took the boys hands in her own. They were perfect. The toes sticking out of his sandals were perfect. She ran her fingers over his ears, touched his nose. Everything about him was just as it should be.

"Tiras told us you went back home to your family," Ethan said. "Your parents were overjoyed to see you, yes? Are they here with you?"

"They don't want me any more," the boy replied, his head bowed to hide the sudden moisture in his eyes. "They are not sure the leprosy won't come back."

"Surely the priest has seen you and declared you clean. Does that make no difference to them?" Ethan questioned.

"I cannot go into the synagogue because I believe Jesus of Nazareth is the Messiah. So my parents don't want me. They say I am as a dead son to them. Do you need a son? I can work. My fingers are all here. I can do good work."

Chapter 13

JUDITH AND ETHAN exchanged startled, anguished glances. This was too great a decision to make at the edge of a booth.

"Come, you can help us with our work," Ethan suggested. Judith watched as the boy earnestly listened to Ethan's instructions.

Now Judith was eager to seek healing for herself. If this prophet could heal leprosy, he certainly could heal her. What was her pain compared to the ravages of leprosy?

Ethan put the boy to work and he willingly did anything he was asked to do. Before long they were creating jobs for him and sending him on errands.

"Didn't you hear?" Someone sneered when Judith finally asked about Jesus. "He's afraid of the Pharisees. He isn't coming to the city." Judith turned away, disappointed. Her dream crumbled. The pain seemed to intensify as her hope diminished.

The days dragged even though their sales were brisk. At every turn Reuben was there, worshipping them with his brown eyes. He folded rumpled blankets and robes and helped customers tie their purchases onto their animals. His fingers were agile, even with knots he had almost forgotten. Judith found herself often at the point of running her fingers through his soft curls, wanting to gather this sad creature into her arms. Each time she held back. At night, Reuben chose to curl up in his usual spot by the inn, keeping watch over their booth, he told them.

"You are kind people," he told them. "You used to put coins into my bowl instead of throwing them on the ground." Judith's heart wept. They could have and should have done so much more.

ETHAN CAME RUNNING breathlessly into their stall a few days later. "The prophet is in the city. He's teaching in the temple," he gasped. "You have to go and see him, Judith. I know he can heal you."

Suddenly, Judith was hesitant. "What about the things we've heard?" Judith asked, torn between the Law and her heart's desire. "The Pharisees said he healed on the Sabbath and that was wrong."

"He explained that. He didn't break the law. He only broke some of the *fences* the Pharisees have put up around the law. What he said makes sense." Ethan paced back and forth as he patiently explained what he had heard.

"The Pharisees are trying so hard to protect us from breaking the law that they have made fences, *Seyag,* guaranteed to keep us a safe distance from breaking the Sabbath. Look at their outrageous law that says a tailor has sinned if he forgets and carries a needle pinned to his cloak on the Sabbath!

"The law says we must circumcise on the eighth day even if the eighth day happens to be a Sabbath, so we circumcise on the Sabbath. Isn't that work?" Ethan gestured wildly in his excitement. "We would be breaking the law if we circumcised on the seventh or the ninth day." Judith listened intently, trying to understand, yet fearful of these new ideas. Somehow it made sense, somehow it didn't.

"Look at the handwashing ritual before we eat," he continued. "The Pharisees have heaped so many Traditions of the Fathers upon us that now the water has to be poured, using certain vessels and suitable water in a measured amount. Only specific people can pour it and the hands must be lifted in the air so the water will run down to the wrists. It is only these traditions Jesus breaks, never the Law itself."

Ethan paused and watched in silence as Judith tried to process all that she had heard. "I want we should go and see if this man from Nazareth can heal you."

Judith glanced over at Reuben. He was almost trembling with eagerness. Finally Judith assented.

"For you, I'll go."

They left Reuben in the stall with Tiras, both of them nodding in agreement at their decision to seek out the prophet. The streets were streaming with people as they neared the temple. Judith felt as if the crowd was deliberately keeping them from reaching their destination. Finally they were at a complete standstill. At the center of the crowd they saw the man they sought, the man named Jesus. He was the reason for the crowd and they followed his every move, clamoring for his attention. Many of them Pharisees. Ethan and Judith watched and listened to everything, hesitating to press their case. The Pharisees seemed to be the most attentive listeners, piously clutching the fronts of their robes.

"If this man can heal and calm the storm, what else can he do?" Judith wondered. "Perhaps if he heals me, Jehovah will have mercy and give me a child in my old age, like he did for Sarah." Judith looked around at the blind, the deaf, the crippled. How could she trouble the prophet when many others were so needy?

"I believe he can heal me but what should I do? Do I rush up to him and ask him to do it?" Questions bounced around in her mind. She watched him straighten withered hands and heal other people with a touch. Still she hesitated. Ethan, with his hand on her back, steered her towards the prophet, pushing her through the people. Then, unexpectedly, Judith made eye contact with Jesus. Stopping suddenly he gently laid his hand on her head, and then turned and walked away without saying a word.

Judith stood still, rooted to the spot.

As Jesus and the crowd moved away from her Ethan opened his mouth to call the man back. He looked at his wife, wondering why she had stopped. Then he saw her astonished face.

"It's gone! The pain is gone!" Judith stretched her arms above her head, twisting to each side. She bent to touch her toes, a look of sheer amazement on her face.

Ethan's face lit up with delight and he raced after the prophet. "Thank you! Thank you!" He called over the clamor of the crowd. Quickly he ran back to where Judith waited. They could hardly wait to get to the temple to give thanks to the Lord. The joy of healing eclipsed everything else. They almost flew back to the inn.

Reuben was ecstatic when he heard that Jesus had healed Judith. "I knew Jesus could do it." He danced in circles around the stall. "Jesus can do anything! He's the Messiah, yes?"

Judith stilled. Was that man really the long-awaited Messiah? Yes! He must be. Who but God could heal with a touch?

"Careful who you say that to," Ethan advised the boy. "You don't want to offend our Jewish leaders. They could make trouble for you."

"What can they do to me?" The boy pointed out. "They have already put me out of the synagogue, me, who only last year did my bar mizvah. My parents don't want me. What more could they do?" The sincerity in his voice achieved much more than the words he spoke.

"Just be careful," Ethan repeated. Ethan and Judith lay awake long into the might, talking, praising the Lord. Then they slept as dead people, dreamless and totally at peace.

"May the final verdict be favorable," people called in greeting to one another as the last long blowing of the Ram's Horn brought the festival to an end. Judith knew what they meant. May your sins be cast into the deepest sea in response to your repentance. Judith, for the first time in years, felt that the verdict must be favorable. She was whole again and the Messiah had come.

A twinge of sadness shot through her as they left Reuben in the city to work for Tiras. The fact that Reuben's family had rejected him tore at her heart. "How could any parent do that to their son? What will happen to the boy?" she asked Ethan apprehensively when they got out of hearing. Her feelings for the lad confused her.

Ethan chose to keep his secret from her for now. He had given Tiras a good sum of money to pay the boy's way. He still puzzled over the quizzical look Tiras gave him as he accepted the money.

Judith and Ethan couldn't stop talking about what had happened as they traveled home with their friends. Jacob and Hannah smiled at their excitement, not even aware of what Judith was healed of. She had seldom talked to them about her pain. Even the chill of a winter rain did not change their happy mood. They pulled woolen shawls over their heads and continued describing the event.

"I can hardly believe it." Hannah asked over and over exactly how it had happened. "He didn't even talk to you? Did you know that he healed a blind man too?"

"He spat on the ground and made a paste to put on the man's eyes," Jacob contributed, turning to look over his shoulder at the women. "You remember that man who used to beg by the temple? That's the one."

"He healed the young leper boy who always sat by the inn," Ethan added, "and he healed Judith." Hannah and Jacob realized that there was something new between this couple, something that had been missing for a long time. Was it the healing or something more?

"Perhaps you should be careful about what you say when we get back to Bethlehem," Jacob said to his friends. Ethan and Judith looked at him in shock, hearing an echo of almost the exact words Ethan had spoken earlier to Reuben. "I heard that one man who was healed has been put out of the synagogue. You remember that anyone who believes that Jesus of Nazareth is the Messiah will not be allowed into the synagogue? As your friend, I beg of you to be careful."

"But what if he is the Christ?" Judith asked. Hannah and Jacob gasped. Ethan looked at his wife and gently shook his head. Judith realized that such thoughts must be kept to herself. She looked at Hannah and laughed, pulling her robe closer to keep out the cold wind. The tension broke and the four of them continued their journey home as the chill wind of politics continued to blow in their land.

It was harder to keep their thoughts to themselves when Ethan's mother began to interrogate them. Every year the woman seemed to shrink with age and her hair was now snow white. She watched Judith bustle around the house when they returned. Usually Judith would have to rest after the trip and the woman would grab her parcels, make a few disparaging remarks under her breath and leave. Today she lingered, not hearing sufficient answers to all her questions. Ethan finally went up onto the housetop.

"Maybe your pain will get so bad you will die. Then Ethan can take another wife and have a son," she said in a loud whisper when Ethan was out of hearing. This was a statement the old woman made every chance she had. She lived for the day Ethan would get another wife. It grated on her that Judith was still around. She watched Judith like a hawk, always hoping the pain was worse and death just around the corner.

Today Judith did not sit down to rest. Instead, she gathered her supplies to make cheese blintzes. Having mixed the batter, she poured a little at a time into a hot pan, swirling it around to make a thin crepe. She twisted as she slipped each one out of the pan to cool. She turned back and forth until she soon had a nice pile.

The old woman watched her finish the thin pancakes, and then stir up the filling of cheeses mixed with eggs and raisins. Alya's eyes narrowed as Judith filled each pancake, rolled it up and tucked in the ends. When Judith began to sauté the rolled pancakes until they were brown and crispy, a sneer crossed the old woman's face."You found some new herbs to take away your pain, yes?" She bluntly demanded to know.

Judith hesitated, not wanting to get into a verbal war with the woman, and one would surely arise when the truth came out. She continued to sauté cheese blintzes, placing them side by side on the table to cool.

"What has happened? Something has happened that you aren't telling me." Ayla's voice rose in indignation and anger.

"A prophet healed Judith when we were in Jerusalem," Ethan stated, coming down from the rooftop just then and helping himself to a cheese blintz.

Chapter 14

"No! No! No! Not that horrible man from Nazareth," the woman screeched. "That man is no prophet. He's from Galilee. He breaks all the laws. He's putting us all in danger. If someone doesn't stop him, God forbid, the Romans will take our land away from us. How could you be so stupid?" Her hands shook with rage. Her dream of a new wife for Ethan had just been shattered.

"We only know what happened," Ethan replied calmly. "Jesus touched Judith and the pain is gone. No ordinary man can do that."

"You are a disgrace to our family," his mother raved on, looking at Judith. "You cannot give us more grandchildren to receive our inheritance, and now you lead our son astray too." Turning to Ethan she ranted. "We named you Ethan because it means *firmness, perpetuity*. What good did that do? You have not perpetuated the family and you cannot even be firm with your wife. You, a descendent of Judah, tribe of Zerah, family of Gershom. Look at your wife. A disgrace to us and so are you."

Ethan, crushed by his mother's bruising words, placed his arm around his wife. He would not dishonor his mother by talking back to her, but in this way he would indicate that he stood by his beloved Judith.

The older woman stared at them for a few seconds, then turned and stalked out the door.

"Is it possible that this Jesus is just another rebel trying to raise a following to overthrow the Romans?" Judith asked after the door had closed. "Remember the man named Judas who led a movement six years before the census? The one they killed?"

"Judith, how can you think that? This man does all these miracles in his own power, you think? He has the power of God with him. He healed you, yes?" Ethan placed his hands on Judith's upper arms, holding her still, calming her down.

"You're right. I know he's different but I just don't understand how or why."

"Come, it's time for us to put up our booth for the Feast of Tabernacles." Ethan led her by the hand to the rooftop where they would build the temporary structure. "For the seven days of the feast, let's just forget about everything else and just enjoy camping in our *sukkah*. Let's praise Jehovah for the final in-gathering of the harvest. It was a good harvest, yes? We have a lot to praise him for this year."

They built the booth on top of the house, covering it loosely with branches so both the sun and the rain could come in. Judith stretched as she handed the branches up to Ethan, savoring the freedom.

"I can't imagine our forefathers spending forty years in the wilderness living like this," she stated later as she decorated the inside of the booth with flowers and fruits, the red pomegranates adding a festive atmosphere there on the rooftop. "Imagine, a whole generation of children who had never been inside a solid building. Jair would have loved this."

"We should sleep up here for at least one night," Ethan suggested. Judith smiled, knowing they would sleep there every night and watch the stars shine through the branches. She remembered when Jair was a toddler and they looked forward to showing him the star-filled night. He fell asleep before dark and slept all night. How she had anticipated the fun they would have as he grew up.

"Maybe the evenings will be cool enough to keep the gnats away; we should have such luck," Judith said with a chuckle, remembering past years when they had to retreat into the house before they were eaten alive.

Judith prepared a place for them to eat in the booth, laughing and joking with Ethan. As a child she had loved this celebration with her own parents. Now Judith happily gathered what she needed to bake fruit and vegetable *kugel*. One of their traditions, the *kugel* would add to the joyous atmosphere of the feast days. The whole village became one as they sang and danced away the hours, munched on a variety of sweets. Music and laughter echoed over the rooftops.

Judith and Ethan loved this time when the the soft glow of lamplight radiated from each housetop and a sense of oneness settled over the village.

✡ ✡ ✡

"Where did you put the palm and citron branches?" Ethan asked as they prepared to walk to the synagogue. The tangy scent of the citron filled the room as Judith brought them from the courtyard. Every day they joined the rest of the community in a procession, waving the palm and citron branches and chanting psalms. The last day of the feast, the crowning day of all their feast days, they repeated the procession seven times. The next day Ethan dismantled the booth and put it away until the next year.

"Every day I praise Jehovah that I am free of pain and able to do my share of the work," Judith stated, as shearing time came again. This year she could do some of the jobs that were difficult for Noam in his old age. Ayla and Nina kept them well-fed and day after day the pile of fleeces grew. This year, she would add new colors to her blankets and robes. She would dye more yarn than ever before. The Lord had renewed her strength and she could hardly wait to prove it.

Every kettle they owned, and a few borrowed from Ayla, almost filled the courtyard. Judith kept a close eye on the kettles as water simmered over the outdoor hearth. She had developed a wide variety of colors using various plants that she had collected during the year and this year she would even experiment with some combinations. She threw onion skins into one pot and the water soon turned a warm rust color. She tossed yellow flowers into another pot of water, producing a yellow dye bath. Berries yielded a soft blue. Placing the wool in these pots, she simmered them until they were the colors she wanted. Judith sang as she worked with the dyes. She added red poppies to the yellow water to make a rich orange dye. Oak bark gave her shades of brown and various grasses gave her a variety of green shades. After she had finished with one color she had to reheat water to begin another color. Judith was careful not to agitate the wool in the dye bath, gently lifting the heavy, dripping skeins from the pots with a strong stick, and hanging them up to dry. She delighted in the colorful flower garden of wool that grew before her eyes.

Ethan hovered in another part of the house. For several years he had taken time from his own work to help with this task. Silently he peeked to make sure she was able to cope and then, with a huge grin creasing his face, he was gone.

For three days Judith dyed wool, then waited impatiently for the skeins to dry.

"Ethan, remember when I told you about the purple dye from Tyre? I am going to make enough money, God willing, so I can buy some next year."

"I seem to remember it, but remind me what that dye is."

"A white secretion is milked from the murex sea snail," Judith explained. "It's very expensive but it's amazing. When it's rubbed into a garment it turns the most beautiful purple. God willing, next year I'll be weaving with purple too. Just think of the robes I could make with that." Ethan smiled as he thought of the people wanting to purchase those! Purple robes, symbol of royalty!

"With all your energy and enthusiasm we'll soon be rich enough to buy anything we want." Ethan grabbed his wife and danced her across the floor until they were both weak with laughter.

"I can't wait any longer for the wool to dry. I'm going to start weaving with undyed wool. Maybe by the time I'm ready to weave the pattern some of the colors will be dry." She threaded white wool through the heddles of her loom and began weaving her favorite design, a pattern so old it had probably come with Moses from Egypt.

They were comfortable and contented together with Ethan relaxed nearby, content to watch, but ready to help if she needed him. Judith wouldn't even mind when the winter rains began pelting down and the sky remained dull and heavy for weeks at a time. She had plenty of wool to spin and weave, and the endurance to match. She did everything faster these days. Her trips to the well for their drinking water were no effort at all. She expended an amazing amount of energy as she scrubbed their clothes and hauling the wet laundry home, and hanging it was no longer a chore for her.

Ethan woke a few weeks later to pots being banged in the kitchen and the delicious smell of breakfast being prepared. "This smells good," Ethan stated as he sat down at the table. Judith already had an egg and tomato scramble set out and she quickly added slices of grapefruit, bread and orange marmalade.

"I put falafel and fruit in your bag for midday." She quickly dished food onto his plate and sat back to wait for the blessing." Ethan's morning routine was to check each of the animals for illness or injury as they came out of the sheepfold beneath his parents' home. His mother usually had the morning milking done when he got there, since they milked only two goats, providing her with a little income of her own. This job she never allowed Nina to do. Today he got the impression that Judith was in a hurry for him to leave.

"What have you got planned today?" he asked with a puzzled expression.

"I'm going to spend all day at the loom." With that, Judith jumped up from the table and plucked Ethan's dish out from under his nose as he put the last bite of food in his mouth. She bustled about the room. She fidgeted as Ethan drank the last of his juice. Finally she blurted out what had been on her mind for days, even weeks.

"Ethan, would you mind if I made something for Reuben? Maybe a warm robe for him for winter? I don't know where he gets his clothes." Ethan calmed her with a hug.

"I think that would be great," he whispered in her ear. Loosing his grip on his wife he continued. "I wonder if he has a sling? I could make him one, but that might not be such a good idea in the city. Would he be too old for a wooden cart to haul things around on?" He was still coming up with ideas as Judith pushed him out the door, putting his lunch in his hand.

Since they had had neither meat nor dairy for breakfast, it didn't take her long to clean up after the meal. A robe she had finished the evening before lay folded across the loom but it was quickly folded and added to the pile behind the door. Next she looked through her piles of spun wool. If everything went as planned she could be weaving by early afternoon. But then if something went wrong, like tangled threads, setting up the loom could take a good part of the day. Judith's heart was so full of praise that nothing would bother her today. She chose some exceptionally fine, sand-colored wool. She praised Jehovah that she had no pain now when she wound the yarn around the two stakes Ethan had pounded in the floor for her. As she worked she thought about Reuben and Jesus and her own healing.

"There's no doubt that Jesus is a great teacher and miracle worker but can he really be the Messiah?" Judith questioned as she worked. When she had as much yarn on the stakes as she needed, she inserted a rod into each end and carried the yarn to the loom. Judith calculated how wide this robe should be for a boy's frame as she fastened one end of the yarn to the crossbeam Ethan had made so many years ago. Weaving the smaller robe would not take very long.

Her mind was busy recalling everything she had learned about the prophet from Nazareth. "I certainly don't have the faith that young Reuben has, but he's young. He's so convinced this man is the Messiah." It seemed as if she had as many questions as there were warp threads woven through the heddles.

"I wonder what Jacob thinks about Jesus?" He had come to mind as she had fastened the wool to the small pottery disks to pull the thread taut. Jacob had traded them for one of the warm robes she wove. "Sometimes he seems to believe and at other times he seems afraid."

When she finally sat down to weave every movement came automatically, from years of practice. Her feet on the pedals moved the heddles, opening first one tunnel or shed, and then the opposite one. Judith deftly slid the shuttle through, pulled the beater bar to pack that horizontal weft thread in place, raised the opposite heddles and slid the shuttle back through the new tunnel. Swoosh! Thud! Swoosh! Thud! The shuttle and the beater bar added a drum-like cadence to the day and every row was as neat and tight as the one before it.

This robe was special so Judith had not only taken her time choosing the colors, but had also designed a new pattern as she wove in the colors.

Up and down, back and forth. The rhythm of the loom soon had Judith singing with the beat, and all the time she thought about the prophet. Now and then excitement about the possible Messiah made her stomach lurch but some things, like his place of birth, confused her.

Ethan, meanwhile, called each of the sheep out of the sheepfold and remembered the last time he and Judith had been in Jerusalem. He wondered if Reuben would like to come here to Bethlehem sometime and see the sheep. Jesus had talked about sheep. The discussion had completely slipped his mind, but now he remembered and suddenly he had an urge to go with his father to the pasture. He had many things on his mind and it was a private place where they could talk.

Chapter 15

"YOU ARE A perfect example of a shepherd," Ethan told his father as they climbed the hill. "The last time we were in Jerusalem, Jesus from Nazareth declared that he was the good shepherd." The elderly man, his hair almost white, nodded his head, weighing every word his son spoke.

"I wonder why Jesus called himself the good shepherd when everyone knows he is a carpenter? Everything he said about the care of sheep was correct, too," Ethan continued. "How could Jesus know so much about sheep?" They came to a green meadow where the flock could graze and his father found a convenient rock where he could rest his calloused feet.

"Perhaps he is a very wise man and learns quickly," his father suggested. "On the other hand, perhaps he is the Messiah and has exceptional wisdom from Jehovah."

Ethan was stunned to hear his father speak this way. "Do you think so? Does that bother you? Do you not feel the same way Mother does about him?" Ethan concentrated on picking up some small stones and loaded his sling, so he wouldn't have to look at his father. Ethan chose a distant bush as he waited for his father's reply. He sent a stone sailing through the air and the bush shook. His father joined him, swinging his own sling with precision, his aim as accurate as ever. If ever a predator came after their sheep, they were always prepared.

"All my life I have waited for the Messiah," Noam finally replied. "I would die a happy man if I lived to meet the Messiah."

"The crowds follow the prophet wherever he goes just like the sheep follow you," Ethan told his father.

"Perhaps that's what he means, that he is like a shepherd to the people."

Ethan realized how feeble his father was getting after a long life of hard work, yet his mind was as sharp as ever. It thrilled him to know they could talk openly about such a controversial issue. The fact that he had no grandchildren weighed heavily on the old man. He had Ethan to claim the inheritance but after that there was no one to carry on the family name, a disgrace amongst their people. That was a topic they had never discussed.

Ethan's shoulders sagged with responsibility. Whatever he did he would be letting down either his parents or his wife. There was nothing he could do for his parents short of taking another wife. He could never do that. He could relate to the stoop of his father's shoulders. Then, suddenly a thought came to his mind. He wondered if young Reuben liked sheep.

"Someday I would like to bring a young friend of ours here to see the sheep," Ethan blurted out. "He was a leper begging in Jerusalem but Jesus healed him. Last year he did his bar mitzvah but now he is banned from the synagogue because he believes Jesus is the Messiah." Ethan looked directly at his father, trying to discern his response. The old man's eyes shone. Ethan realized he would welcome a youngster around the place. His mother's response would be another matter.

Ethan left his father in the hills with the flock and returned home, stopping first to see his mother and his cousin, Nina. He didn't stay long when Nina told him his mother had gone to his house. Usually he enjoyed visiting with Nina, but today his pace quickened as he headed for home. He rushed through the streets, his robes billowing out behind him.

Judith had just started to weave in the colors when her mother-in-law arrived. In the past the two women had gradually sorted out the jobs and spent years working in the same room combing wool, spinning, dyeing it and weaving. Some days had been peaceful and full of conversation. Others had been filled with tension and silence. They shared the chore of combing and each did some of the spinning, but Judith did all the dyeing and weaving.

"I think I will take my spindle home and work there." Ethan's mother stood in the center of the room, waiting for a response.

Thunk! Thunk! Judith continued to work on the loom. *What's upset her this time?* she wondered. Over the years the woman had threatened to take everything home and work by herself whenever Judith upset her. *Personally*, Judith thought, *I would just as soon the woman did go home but for Ethan's sake I'll do what I can to placate his mother.*

"Is it easier to carry all the wool back to your house?" Judith asked. "Sit here and rest your feet." Ayla pretended to sort through the spun wool, sending the skeins bouncing and flying around. She didn't touch the colored wool by the loom and ignored the rolags. Her jawbones moved as she clenched and unclenched her teeth. Her lips moved, preparing to form the words that were in her mind. The tension in the room continued to build.

Judith, distracted, misjudged the shed and got the shuttle tangled going through the shed. Suddenly, the loom was quiet. Judith gnawed on her inner lip, willing herself not to speak. The explosion was close when Ethan burst through the door. He paused, looking from one to the other, and breathed a sigh of relief. He was in time; the battle had not begun. He would stand as a buffer between the two women he loved.

"Your mother wants to take her wool and work at home," Judith stated quietly. She didn't want to fight with Ethan's family but it rankled her when guilt drove her to give in. Today she felt truly sorry for the old woman, drowning in a cesspool of hate of her own making. Judith stared expectantly at Ethan. Sensing Judith's change of heart, he walked over to put his arm around his mother.

"You don't really want to do that," he said. "Stay and spin. Keep me company. I need to oil some straps anyway and I'll visit with you." With a toss of her head and a sly satisfied glance at Judith, the woman picked up the spindle, tied a length of wool from her distaff onto it and began to spin. The spindle slowly lowered to the floor as the wool played out. Ethan sat down with his straps and a dish of olive oil.

Thankful that it was warm enough to be outside, Judith went up to the rooftop, leaving the two of them to visit in private. She could hear the murmur of their conversation and marveled at Ethan's patience.

"Stay away from that Galilean," the woman said, her voice suddenly loud and piercing. "He's nothing but trouble. There are all kinds of rumors about him. He is a rabble-rouser, just like all the others before him."

Judith smiled, not at the words, but because they were meant to reach her ears.

"He is going to be the downfall of our nation if he continues to stir up the people. What does he know? He's from Galilee." The shrill voice carried up to the rooftop and beyond.

"He seems to be a very learned man," Ethan replied quietly. "He keeps all the laws. He only breaks the Pharisees' fences. Is that so bad?"

"Why do you think the *seyag* are there? They are put there to protect. If he goes that far, sooner or later, he will break the Law too. Just stay away from him!"

To avoid an argument, Ethan did not reply. Ethan would never let his mother know that the prophet intrigued him and he certainly would never tell her what his father thought about the man.

Chapter 16

JUDITH PUT THE finishing touches on the smaller robe. The colors were a bit brighter and she took great care with the detail. When it was done she set it apart from the others.

Ethan began spending more time with his father on the hills. He also took every opportunity to listen to the wise and respected Pharisees, as did all the men in Bethlehem. The Pharisees inhabited their own community within the village but they also carried a wealth of news from one town to another. As he listened to the Pharisees discuss the travels and deeds of Jesus, Ethan purposely kept his expression unchanged, careful to hide what he really thought.

If his mother knew how he felt about the man she would blame Judith, just as she blamed Judith for everything else that went wrong. If the Pharisees knew his thoughts, the consequences would be much worse.

Then one day Ethan heard news that startled him more than usual.

"The situation is serious," one of the Pharisees stated. "This Galilean was in Bethany a few days ago and claims to have raised a man from the dead, a man named Lazarus."

"That's impossible," someone yelled. "No one can bring the dead back to life."

"That's what I said," the older Pharisee replied. "But the people in Bethany are stirred up about it. The man and his sisters all tell the same story: 'The man got sick. His sisters called Jesus to come, hoping he could heal him but he didn't get there in time. Lazarus died. Everyone who was there agrees that he was dead for several days and beginning to stink already.'"

"Then Jesus came into Bethany and called Lazarus to come out of the tomb," another Pharisee added. "At least that's what the people say. He came out wrapped in burial clothes, reeking of death. Now if he were not really dead, would he stink?" Everyone began to talk at once, debating the possibility.

"If he were already dead, how could anyone raise him to life again?" This led to an even noisier and heated debate.

Ethan stood silently on the edge of the crowd, amazed at what he was hearing. He wondered if this had actually happened. The Galilean had healed Judith, Reuben and many others. He had calmed a storm with his words. If he could do all that, then maybe he could raise someone from the dead too. Ethan almost gasped aloud at his own thoughts. If Jesus did raise someone from the dead, perhaps, just perhaps, this man was the Messiah.

"If any of you know where this prophet from Galilee is, you must tell us. This situation is getting dangerous.

More and more people follow him. If we don't get rid of him the Romans will do away with him, and with us, for not stopping him. They will take back the responsibilities they have allowed us to handle and after that every part of our lives, even our spiritual lives will be controlled by the Romans. It is imperative that we put this man to death, and also Lazarus, whom he supposedly raised from the dead."

The entire time he was speaking the Pharisee was getting louder and louder. One by one, the people surrounding him began to mutter as this final statement resounded over the rumblings and shouts from the crowd.

Stunned, Ethan glanced around, watching the response from the crowd. He saw Jacob watching him. Jacob would be wondering what his reaction would be to this latest news. This kind of excitement was nothing new amongst his people but it was different this time. They were talking of killing someone he knew.

"That's interesting news," Jacob said, catching up with Ethan on his way home. "What do you think about it?"

"I don't know. Do you think a man could bring a dead person back to life?"

"There are rumors that this isn't the first one he has raised from the dead," Jacob said quietly.

Ethan glanced quickly at his friend to see if he was serious. Jacob was looking directly at him.

"I hadn't heard that."

"Be careful, Ethan. If the Pharisees hear that you had anything to do with the man they might come looking for answers from you. I've heard the Sanhedrin has made a final decision to put him to death. They are the recognized leaders of our people. Be careful, friend." Jacob squeezed Ethan's shoulder as he left him at the corner of his street.

Ethan thought about the Sanhedrin, seventy members - Priests, Sadducean nobles, some Pharisees, Scribes and Elders, with the High Priest presiding over them all. Would they or could they put to death one of their own fellow countrymen?

Ethan walked through the narrow streets deep in thought. He heard children playing inside open doors, babies crying, and women talking together across the rooftops. None of that turned his thoughts from what he had just heard from the Pharisees.

Suddenly the sound of his mother's voice pulled him abruptly back to reality. He quickened his pace. He could hear her voice raised in rebuke as he approached his house, and immediately, he knew that she had also heard the news. He could not understand how news could travel so fast.

"Just wait until Ethan comes home." He heard his mother's strident voice as he approached the door. "He'll have heard all about it; he'll tell you it's not true." Ethan pushed the door open and walked into the room. His mother and his wife stood facing each other like David and Goliath. The tension was palpable.

"Ethan, what have you heard?" His mother demanded. "Do people think we are so stupid as to believe this Galilean raised someone from the dead? Tell us, what is this nonsense? No one but Jehovah himself could do that."

"Who am I to decide what is true?" Ethan replied. "I am only the messenger. That is what people are saying. Jesus of Nazareth raised Lazarus of Bethany from the dead four days after he died. They say he had already begun to stink. I even heard that he has raised others from the dead before that." His mother's face turned red and her eyes narrowed.

"Everyone is also talking about the Sanhedrin's decision. If the Sanhedrin has decided to be rid of him, it is as good as done," she stated emphatically. "Who would ever believe all these lies and rumors? No one but God can raise the dead!"

Judith almost laughed with glee at what the woman had just said. Did the woman not realize she had just put Jesus on an equal level with Jehovah if, indeed, he did raise this man? Ethan took the brunt of her continued verbal abuse this time and finally walked her home.

The almonds were in full bloom and their scent filled the evening air. Spring rains would be falling any day and soon it would be Passover, then time for the flax and barley harvest.

Ethan listened avidly each day for more news about Jesus and discussed it with Judith, and privately with his father, but none of them talked to anyone else about what they heard.

Judith spent hours thinking about all these things as she sat at the loom. Ethan, in his preparations for their next trip to the city, picked up a robe to add to his bundle. Holding it up, he looked at it for a long time. Then he folded it again and he too set this smaller robe apart from the rest of the garments. A smile played over his lips. Judith was in the other room. Ethan never mentioned it to her but went about his work with a light heart.

✡ ✡ ✡

"JUDITH! I HEARD that the prophet from Galilee is in Bethany visiting his friends," Ethan said breathlessly as he came into the house. He had been listening to the news brought to town by travelers as he went about his business. He had rushed to get home but fifty-plus years had taken their toll on him too and he could not hurry as fast as he once could.

"Perhaps Jesus won't go to Jerusalem for the Passover," Judith replied. "Last time they were looking for him to put him to death. This time they will be watching more closely."

"I know," Ethan continued. "That's why I thought that instead of going right to Jerusalem, we could take the other road and go around through Bethany - that is, if you want to. We could be in Bethany by mid-day, have our meal there and still get to Jerusalem before dark." Judith's eyes lit up. Her mouth moved as she chewed on her lip, deep in thought.

"I don't think we should tell your parents," Judith suggested softly. "If your mother knew what we were planning she would have all kinds of reasons to delay our departure. We could get everything ready this evening and leave early before anyone is up."

"I will tell only my father," Ethan replied. "If there are any questions he can truthfully tell everyone we left early."

"I'll be waiting to hear about your trip," his father diplomatically told him as they talked beside the sheepcote. Ethan put a lead rope on the donkey. He would tie the animal outside their house for the night. His father's hand on his shoulder brought him to a stop. "May Jehovah bless you, my son."

"We'll have to let Jacob and Hannah know that we won't be traveling with them." Ethan said later as he began gathering supplies. "What reason would we give them?"

"Maybe they'd like to go with us. They've seemed interested in all the news about the prophet. Perhaps they secretly believe in him too."

"They might, but Jacob would not risk offending the Pharisees, even if he did believe in this man. I'll tell them the truth. If I ask Jacob not to tell anyone, he won't." Ethan left to find Jacob while Judith arranged food for their trip. Their excitement grew with each passing hour, although they were careful to hide their feelings when Ethan's mother suddenly stopped in, bringing goat's milk.

Judith checked the many containers in which she had food items preserved in brine and chose cucumbers, olives, capers and even melon for them to take along. That would be ample for their mid-day meal and another meal when they arrived in Jerusalem.

Pouring barley onto her grindstone, she ground enough flour to make pitas in the morning. Along with dates, raisins and the preserved food, they would provide filling meals along the way.

Everything was ready by dusk. The robes and blankets, bound together, were ready to load on the donkey. Judith had all their other supplies ready.

Finally, Judith buried eggs in the hot ashes in the hearth just before she went to bed. They would be cooked hard by morning, ready to take with them. When they finally went to bed Judith, deep in thought, curled on her side, not wanting to disturb her sleeping husband. Ethan lay on his back, staring at the ceiling, careful not to wake his sleeping wife. Hours passed before their breathing slowed and deepened in sleep.

"Judith, are you awake?" Ethan whispered as the sky was showing the first light of dawn.

"I have hardly slept all night," she replied immediately. "We might as well get up and go as lie awake." She plucked the eggs from the ashes and quickly lit a fire. Within minutes the pitas were stuck to the inside walls of the clay oven, baking.

Ethan loaded the donkey, balancing the load with precision. In their eagerness to be on the way they decided to eat even their morning meal as they traveled.

Quietly they left the house. Their lungs expanded with fresh morning air as they walked through the narrow streets. All the other homes were silent, their chimneys smokeless. Birds were beginning to welcome the day and a rooster crowed as they left the village behind them. Even the donkey's steps seemed muffled on the packed path. Daisies and poppies dotted the hillsides, and the flax and barley fields, almost ready for harvest, bent heavy heads.

The first part of their journey followed the familiar road to Jerusalem, but when the road divided they branched off, cutting down into the valley. Bethany lay a short distance east of Jerusalem and morning was only half gone when they sighted the small town, the homes terraced on the hilly terrain. Their eagerness to see Jesus caused them to move faster the closer they got to their destination.

Chapter 17

"HOW WILL WE find him?" Judith asked. She soon realized the question was redundant. They had only to listen to the people passing them. He was the topic of conversation all over the village. They found him surrounded as usual by a crowd.

It took them only moments to pick out Lazarus. He was telling his story again as people questioned him, now months after the event. His sisters told of their anguish and grief as their brother got sick and finally died.

Judith relived in her mind the mourning and grief she had gone through when Jair died and her heart went out to these women. She listened, amazed as she heard first hand about his death and burial.

The sisters told their side of the story, how they had wept and waited for Jesus to come. They talked about the hopeless feelings they had had, even when Jesus finally did arrive in their village, too late. Their brother was dead.

"I was there too," another man joined in. "We followed you when you took Jesus to the cave where Lazarus was buried."

"Then he called Lazarus to come out of the tomb."

"I had been in the grave four days already when I heard him call, 'Lazarus, come forth.' The smell of death was strong but I had to obey that voice," Lazarus stated. "The putrid odor clung to the shroud even after they removed it." People plugged their noses and nodded briskly.

Judith and Ethan could hear the astonishment in their voices even yet as people told of Lazarus, walking out of the tomb, still bound in grave clothes.

Judith and Ethan loved listening to the recounting of this great event, but more exciting was the appearance of Jesus himself talking to the crowd. This was the man they had come to see. This was the man who had actually done this great thing. Jesus reminded them that Lazarus's death was meant to bring glory to God. His words imparted knowledge even as he spoke. Judith listened spellbound. This man could raise the dead. This was the man who had healed her. Where did his power come from?

Judith and Ethan stayed as long as they could but the time came when they knew they had to continue into Jerusalem in order to be ready for business the next day. Reluctantly they left the crowd and the town behind.

"I am becoming more and more convinced that this must be the Messiah," Ethan stated as they walked towards the city.

"I am too," Judith added. "The thing is, how can he be the Messiah when he is from Galilee? Your mother said the Messiah must come from Bethlehem, according to Scripture." Then she added with a grin, "For once I agree with your mother."

"But how could he raise a man from the dead and make the wind obey him unless he was the Messiah? My mother also stated," Ethan said, with a chuckle, "that no one could raise the dead but Jehovah himself!" Ethan laughed aloud at the words his mother had uttered, while denying the fact at every turn. The journey into the city passed quickly as they discussed everything they knew about the man."

Reuben burst through the inn door as they came near. He wanted to do everything for them, unload the donkey and set up the booth. Tiras stood in the doorway, a wide smile on his face as he watched the three of them. Then Ethan and Tiras walked into the inn together, deep in conversation. By nightfall everything was ready. Judith and Ethan retired to a room in the inn while Reuben settled down outside, watching the booth. Ethan noticed the lad was snuggled into the robe Judith had made for him.

Business was brisk the next day. Reuben was everywhere at once. He could not seem to keep his hands off the robes and blankets. Judith watched him and thought how wonderful that this lad, who only months before could not feel a thing with his leprous hands, could now enjoy the softness of the wool. She was glad she had put extra care into the robe he now wore.

Judith was showing off one of her best robes when they heard a commotion at one of the city gates - the sound of people singing and yelling in glee. Judging by the sounds reaching them, the crowd was growing as it neared the city.

"I wonder what's going on. Should I run and see?" Judith moved from behind the stall.

"We'll stay here." Ethan nodded his consent.

Judith rushed towards the gate and arrived just in time to see Jesus of Nazareth riding through the gate on a donkey. People shouted and sang, waving branches as the man and a huge following of people paraded past her, the toddlers riding high on their fathers' shoulders. Judith clutched her hands close to her breast in excitement. She couldn't help being caught up in the frenzy. Children ran about excitedly, waving branches and enjoying the whole event. Some of the people threw their coats on the ground for the donkey to walk over.

"Blessed is the King of Israel," people cheered and Judith cheered with those around her as he went by. She followed the crowd, wondering where they were going. Who would not cheer for such a wonderful person, the one who had healed her? The one who had raised the dead! If he were their king, what limits would there be?

"Our King?" This thought reverberated around in Judith's mind. "He would make a wonderful king," she thought. "Just think what he could do for our nation." She cheered more loudly. Picking up a palm branch someone had dropped she entered into the festivities.

"Hosanna!" rang through the streets. "Save us now!" Judith shouted the refrain along with the rest of the crowd. No one seemed to mind that the phrase, usually addressed to Jehovah, was now being shouted at Jesus.

"This is our new king," a man yelled to people watching along the route. "This is the King of the Jews." Judith's hand flew to her throat, her breath suddenly cut off. The phrase going around and around in her mind eclipsed even the sound of the crowd as it carried her along. *This is the King of the Jews.* The palm branch dropped to the ground.

"This is the King of the Jews."

"Do you know this man?" Judith demanded of the one who had made the statement. "Do you know where he was born?"

"I don't know where he was born, but it's Jesus of Nazareth. He must have been born in Nazareth." Judith stumbled from person to person asking the same question and she got the same answer from everyone. No one seemed to know. Finally she found a woman who knew him well.

"He was born in Bethlehem."

The blood drained from Judith's face and her hands shook. Pulling her veil across her stricken face, she turned and staggered away from the procession, fighting against the flow of bodies. On legs weak with shock she stumbled back to the stall where Ethan waited for her.

"What is it, Judith?" Ethan took her shaking hands in his own and sat her down. "What was all the commotion at the gate?"

Reuben backed away when he saw her frightened, tear-streaked face. Slowly he moved outside the stall, giving them privacy, but stayed close by.

"It was Jesus coming into the city." Ethan's brow creased in confusion at her answer. "He is the King of the Jews. He was born in Bethlehem." Judith could no longer hold back the sobs. Ethan's face blanched.

"It can't be." Visibly shaken, he wrapped his arms around his wife and the sobs that shook her body brought forth tears, disbelief and then anger in him. Reuben watched in confusion. How wonderful to see Jesus coming into the city. What had upset Judith so?

"This was the man who was born in Bethlehem when our baby was born," Judith sobbed. "He is the reason our son Jair was killed." Their minds recalled every moment of that horrendous long-ago day, and they felt the debilitating bereavement all over again.

"I don't understand," Judith sobbed. "I just don't understand."

"Reuben, go to Tiras. Tell him I sent you to stay with him," Ethan said as he saw the boy peering at them with widened eyes. Reuben scurried into the inn to find Tiras.

THEY REMAINED IN the city all week, too numb to pack up and go home. It was a week lived in confusion. Reuben sensing that his presence was not welcome, spent his time in the inn with Tiras. Tension was building in the city. Contrary to the crowds greeting him as king, there was now even more talk of killing Jesus to spare the nation. When Judith and Ethan heard the news of his arrest they followed the gossip with morbid interest.

"He was betrayed by one of his own followers." Ethan told Judith about that event. "I feel we have been betrayed too, but I don't know who is to blame. I saw Jacob and he refused to look at me. He doesn't know our feelings have changed in the past few days. Reuben's faith in the man is unshakable. He's disappointed in us. I am so confused."

News came through the city almost hourly. The prophet was taken before Caiaphas the High Priest.

"You won't believe what happened to me," Ethan said under his breath as he moved across the booth to stand beside Judith. He had been talking quietly to a man for quite a while and Judith assumed the man planned on buying a robe the next time they came to the city. "That man offered me a sum of money if I would testify against Jesus of Nazareth."

Chapter 18

"WHAT COULD YOU say? We haven't had much contact with him. What did he want you to say? Up until a few days ago most of our contact with him was positive."

"He wanted me to make up a story that would discredit him, to bring false accusation against him. He said they would pay me well."

"What? Right now I despise the prophet but even he deserves a fair trial. We don't need money, but eventually they will find someone who is willing to lie for the sake of coins in their hand." They heard reports of Jesus being mocked and spat upon. They retired for the night but it was another night of little sleep. Judith's troubled, confused mind kept her awake. Ethan lay staring at the ceiling, trying to sort out what was happening.

"Did you hear the latest?" A couple stopped by the booth the next morning. "Jesus of Nazareth has been taken before the governor, Pontius Pilate, to be condemned to death."

"The Pharisees are frightened," Ethan replied. "When the people greeted Jesus a few days ago as royalty, they probably were afraid the Romans would take back all their power or worse. If they said nothing it would be as if they condoned the following he has amassed."

"They falsely accused him."

"So they did find someone to do their dirty work?"

"When Pilate asked him to defend himself against his accusers he said nothing. Someone said he was as silent as a sheep being sheared. Pilate already promised to release one prisoner on this festival and offered the people the choice, Jesus of Nazareth or Barabbas."

"Barabbas? That scoundrel? There is no choice to make there. Jesus has so many followers I'm sure they chose Jesus to be released." Ethan and Judith waited to hear the couple answer, knowing full well that the people would choose Jesus.

"They chose Barabbas! Jesus, they sentenced to death! By crucifixion!"

Judith and Ethan stood stunned as the couple moved away. Judith, suddenly chilled to the bone, wrapped her robe tightly around herself. Ethan turned away, his head bowed in defeat. Their feelings left them both confused, wanting him to die because of their son's death, yet at the same time, incensed at the unjust sentence.

"I don't care. Maybe this is Jehovah's way of righting a wrong," Judith finally blurted out. "He will finally pay for Jair's death."

"I hate crucifixions," Ethan stated. "But this one I will go to. I want to see what happens. If, and I say if, Jesus is the Messiah, something will happen; he will not be put to death this way." They followed the crowd through the narrow streets of Jerusalem. They hesitated to talk to anyone, not knowing how anyone else felt about the situation.

Ethan, listening to the conversations around them, was able to piece together what had happened the night before: They arrested Jesus in a garden, across the Kidron Valley, on the slope of the Mount of Olives, also known as *the olive press*. Taken to the palace of the high priest in the lower city, the Sanhedrin declared Jesus guilty of blasphemy, a crime deserving death. They did not have the power to condemn someone to death so they sent him to Pilate's palace beside the temple. Learning that he was a Galilean, Pilate sent him to Herod Antipas, who had his palace in the lower city. Herod Antipas sent him back to Pilate who finally, to keep peace with the Jews, sentenced him to death by crucifixion.

The crowd made its way through the North Gate and followed the road to the Hill of Golgotha, just outside the gates of the city.

"Some people are taking a great delight in this," Judith whispered, shocked at what she saw. "How can people enjoy watching someone die?" Two other prisoners faced crucifixion at the same time, the worst degradation possible.

"For some people this is entertainment," Ethan reminded her pointing out people who had spread blankets on the ground and sat down with their lunch, obviously prepared for a long wait. People from every social level mingled together - Romans with their bright red tunics, wealthy people showing off expensive purple on their robes, and others dressed in the plainest of homespun garments – all had gathered in a common interest.

Some had come to see the other two criminals pay for their crimes. There were shouts of rebuke and anger as soldiers pushed the three men into position. A leather pouch of huge nails thumped to the ground. All eyes were focused on the gruesome event as it unfolded.

Every blow of the hammer reverberated in Judith's soul. The screams of the victims sent shivers down her back, making her hair bristle. Some of the blows seemed powered by the anger within her as she remembered the horrible death her son had died. She felt the earth tremble under her feet as each cross dropped into a hole in the ground.

Suddenly, a Roman ran up with a sign which he nailed to the cross on which Jesus hung. Judith felt sick. The sign read, *Jesus of Nazareth. The King of the Jews*. That statement again. It stabbed her like the blade of a knife.

"That takes away any pity I might have had for him!" Judith exclaimed. The words of the ruthless soldiers who had killed her son ran through her mind again. "If this was the new king, he's dead now!"

"King of the Jews!" That phrase had etched itself into her memory over thirty odd years. Were the Romans just paranoid about a Jewish king? Were they trying to finish a job they had bungled years ago, when they had killed her son by mistake?

"Let him suffer!" Judith breathed in defeat. "Let him die like our baby died." Jair's death had been swift but it took hours for the prophet to die. Hours in which people jeered and taunted. Unlike some in the crowd, who seemed to be in a festive spirit, Judith and Ethan sat in silence, huddled together, supporting one another.

A flurry of activity caught Judith's attention. The soldiers who had been in charge of crucifying Jesus were arguing over the clothing taken from him. One item, his robe, seemed to be causing them concern.

"It has no seams," one of the men stated. "Why don't we cast lots for it? It would be a shame to tear it apart." Judith's knowledge of weaving caused her to sit up and take notice. She saw the men hold up the garment.

"Like the High Priest's robe," she whispered, "it has no seams." She watched as they cast lots for it, and the winner walked off, flaunting his prize.

Who made that for him? she wondered. Only a master weaver could have woven that.

Some people stood on the edge of the crowd, arms folded, feet spread in defiance at what was happening. Their faces were expressionless, as if they did not care. Others, close to the cross, crouched in sorrow, tears coursing down their faces, anguish in their eyes.

"You!" Judith sat up abruptly as someone yelled. "You, who are going to destroy the temple and build it in three days, save yourself. Come down from the cross if you are the Son of God." Judith watched to see what the reaction would be. If Jesus really was the Messiah he should be able to save himself. This was the moment Ethan was waiting for. They held their breath in anticipation. Jesus did not respond.

Then the chief priests, with the scribes and elders, started talking loudly. "He's the King of Israel! Let him come down now from the cross and we will believe him. He trusts in God. Let God rescue him now if he wants him, for he said, *I am the Son of God.*" Jesus did not respond to them either.

Judith's head jerked up as the man on the center cross finally spoke.

"Dear woman, here is your son."

Scanning the crowd, Judith finally saw the woman he was talking to. "That must be his mother," she thought. "What anguish she must be going through to see her son die like this." Tears streaked the woman's cheeks but there was no tension in her body. She seemed at peace.

Judith wondered which was worse, to have your son die as an infant and never see him grow or to watch him grow to manhood, only to have him meet a criminal's death. Her thoughts moved on to what she knew about the man on the cross. "Would a mother know if her son was the Messiah? If he was and she knew, wouldn't she do something to stop this?"

The sky turned ominously dark, yet it was too early for darkness to descend. Some people left in fear, scurrying back inside the city gates.

"Should we go?" Ethan asked. "It's getting chilly."

"I want to stay until I know he's dead," Judith replied. They waited another three hours.

"Father, into your hands I commit my spirit." Jesus of Nazareth spoke and his head dropped forward in death.

"Ethan!" Judith grasped her husband's hand as the ground trembled beneath them and they clung to each other. Judith huddled under her shawl. People cried out in fear and ran for shelter, expecting the heavens to open up and the rain to fall.

They had seen what they came to see. The man was dead but his death did not ease the anger or confusion for Judith and Ethan.

"I guess that proves he wasn't the Messiah," Judith thought aloud.

"It was as if he willed his spirit to leave. In spite of all the wonderful things he did for other people, even healing you, he is dead."

"It's too late for us to leave the city. We'll have to stay until after the Passover. Do we have food for a few more days?"

"If we hurry we can buy some *falafel* at one of the booths. That will have to do." They hurried back into town. Judith could not understand the mixture of feelings that coursed through her. She took one last look at the man hanging on the cross before she entered the city gates. She felt sick.

They caught just one glimpse of Reuben as they neared the inn. His face was twisted in grief.

"He was so sure Jesus was the Messiah," Ethan said quietly. "I don't know what to say to him." Neither Judith nor Ethan could comfort him. They had none to give.

"Someone took Jesus' body and buried it," Tiras told them later in the inn. "The chief priests and the Pharisees were still not satisfied. They went again to Pilate and asked him to secure the tomb. So the tomb was sealed with his own signet. Guards were placed outside to keep watch."

"What do they expect to happen?" Ethan questioned. "The man is dead. He might have raised Lazarus, but who is going to raise him? Do they think he can raise himself from the dead?"

The uproar on the day of the crucifixion was nothing compared to the uproar the day they packed to go home. Rumors were flying. The body of Jesus was gone. The Pharisees and the Romans believed someone had stolen it. Others said the prophet was alive again, raised from the dead by Jehovah himself.

"If that is true, we would know he is the Messiah," Judith stated, "but why would Jehovah send a Messiah and then allow him to die?"

"How could anyone steal the body away when the tomb was sealed and guards were keeping watch?" Ethan asked. Almost reluctantly, they left Jerusalem. The trip home was long; each was caught up in his own thoughts. It was a trip of depression, back to a home that had once again become a place of despair. Judith focused her attention on Rachel's tomb, as usual, as they passed it.

"Do you know what has happened, Rachel?" Judith murmured. "Everything is so confusing. I don't know what to think." She still had to face an empty house and Ethan's mother.

"I was right all along about that awful man," the woman gloated. "You should have listened to me."

Chapter 19

SLOWLY THEY SLID into their routines again. Ethan went to the gates of Bethlehem daily to hear the latest news. People said that many people had seen Jesus alive but they mentioned it only in whispers. The Pharisees hushed anyone who even hinted at it. For many, it was just an end to the life of another rabble-rouser. For others, there had been something awesome about both his life and his death.

Judith took up her work with a sad heart, dreading the times when her mother-in-law came over.

Ethan and his father kept busy harvesting their small barley crop in the days following. Harvesting always began after Passover and ended exactly at Shavuot, seven weeks later.

Judith and her mother-in-law found themselves together again, grinding the new grain for the two loaves they would offer as a sacrifice. Seven weeks was the length of time it took the Children of Israel to journey from Egypt to Mount Sinai where Jehovah gave them His Law and etched it in stone.

"Even the Hebrew women working as slaves in Egypt had no trouble bearing children," Ethan's mother sneered, as she poured grain onto the grind stone. "What excuse do you have? Why have you done this to our family?"

Judith put all her strength into turning the grind stone, biting back a retort. Hearing the cruel, cutting words pouring from the old woman's mouth, it was hard to remember that they had once enjoyed working together. It was amazing that the woman never gave up taunting her. Judith was glad to see an end to the day. Now she could bury herself in her weaving again.

Slowly the next load of robes and blankets began to pile up, ready to take to Jerusalem. Judith still could not understand why and how Jesus had healed her if the man was not the Messiah. She had no physical pain, no matter how hard she worked. Even the aches and pains of aging seemed to be absent.

Jerusalem overflowed with people and animals when Ethan and Judith returned to the city. A caravan of camels carrying corn and olive oil from Egypt blocked the way where the road from Gaza joined the road from Bethlehem. Judith tried to avoid the camels. They had a tendency to spit when they were in a bad temper. The camels won, so Judith and Ethan settled themselves beside the road until the lumbering animals passed.

Another caravan of papyrus and ivory from Sinai, destined for the northern part of the Roman world was not far behind. Traffic congestion developed as these caravans met those carrying jewels, perfumes and silks from the East towards the southern part of the Empire.

"It looks like everyone with goods to sell has come to the city today," Ethan stated as he finally wound his way through the busy streets, with Judith following in his wake.

"I wish we hadn't come," Judith said emphatically. "I don't think I'll ever forget the last time we were here. It makes me shiver every time I think of watching that crucifixion." The hair on Judith's arms stood up as she shivered.

"I hope I never have to watch another crucifixion either." Ethan veered off towards Tiras's inn. "It's in the past and probably forgotten by everyone as most crucifixions are."

"Will you ever forget it?"

"No. I don't understand what happened but it was something unusual."

By rote they set up the booth and laid out their merchandise. Reuben was nowhere in sight. It didn't take long before people came to look, haggle over prices and eventually buy. Judith's mind was not on selling and she quickly realized she'd better pay attention. The buyers bartered with zeal, looking for every sign of a bargain and would get the best of her if she were not alert.

During a lull in business Judith voiced the question that puzzled her so much. "He couldn't have been the Messiah. Why would Jehovah send the Messiah and then allow Him to die before He redeemed us from the hands of the Romans?"

"I don't know. I'm still trying to understand many of his teachings. Are we wrong to want to be free from the domination of the Romans? They do allow us to worship under their rule."

"There seem to be so many different ways of being free. Jesus healed me and I am free from pain. It's like a freedom I've never known before. When I found out who Jesus was anger bound me tighter than before. The pain of Jair's death returned and again I'm bound in a prison of sorrow. I even drove Reuben away." Judith folded and straightened the robes that people had rummaged through.

"All through the history of our people one leader after another has delivered us from our enemies. If Jesus had led us to freedom from the Romans, do you think other kings would have overpowered us again? It's so confusing. I don't know if we'll ever be free."

"People tried several times to make him our king and He wouldn't allow it," Ethan reminded her. "Each time he walked away. If he was born King of the Jews in Bethlehem, and the Magi from the East recognized him as our king, why didn't he let them crown him? I don't understand any of it either."

Crowds of people milled about and business picked up again. Judith recognized people from Egypt, Asia, Arabia and all places in between. Hawkers and vendors called out in singsong voices, trying to tempt others to buy. Many languages echoed through the narrow streets, which was not unusual with all the tradesmen traveling through, but each culture tried to out-shout each other.

At first they were too busy to notice that the noise and confusion had intensified. Ethan paused to listen, a blanket partially folded in his upraised arms. He heard loud voices, but they were not angry voices, more like people shouting instructions. Judith noticed Ethan's stillness and stopped her work too.

"What's happening?" Ethan yelled at the people passing their stall.

"Just some drunken men," a man replied with scorn from where he leaned against another stall, eating a pomegranate and spitting the seeds into the street. Men, drunk? That was strange at this time of the day. Ethan quickly tucked the remaining garments out of sight. Taking Judith by the hand he led her out of the stall and into the crowd so they could hear better. So many strange things had happened in Jerusalem lately; who knew what this was about?

"How does it happen then, that Jews from every part of the earth are all hearing these men speak the wonders of God each in his own language," someone else questioned? Ethan and Judith listened closely.

One voice resounded above the others, and gradually the men shouting in various languages quieted. The chatter of the surrounding audience stilled and a hush settled over the crowd. Only the occasional snort of an animal or cry of a child penetrated the silence. One man turned to speak to the crowd.

"These men are not drunk," he explained. "God has poured out His Spirit as was spoken by the prophet Joel."

"The Holy Spirit!" Ethan looked at Judith. "John the Baptizer said one would come and baptize not with water but with the Holy Spirit. John said that one was the Son of God!" They pushed through the crowd to get closer. "Who is this man that is speaking?" Ethan asked those around them.

"His name is Peter," came the quick reply, "One of Jesus' followers." Ethan's attention was again riveted on the speaker.

"Men of Israel, listen to this: Jesus of Nazareth was a man accredited by God to you by miracles, wonders and signs, which God did among you through him, as you yourselves know."

Judith drew her veil closer over her face and thought about her own healing. She knew Ethan was remembering too, when he squeezed her hand. Her healing was one of those miracles Peter spoke of.

"This man was handed over to you by God's set purpose and foreknowledge; and you, with the help of wicked men, put him to death by nailing him to the cross. But God raised him from the dead, freeing him from the agony of death, because it was impossible for death to keep its hold on him. God has raised this Jesus to life, and we are all witnesses of the fact." Judith scanned that group, a mixture of refined businessmen and fishermen. Some had hints of gray showing in their hair and beards, some seemed quite young. Then her thoughts were quickly drawn back to Peter as he continued to speak.

"Exalted to the right hand of God, he has received from the Father the promised Holy Spirit and has poured out what you now see and hear. God has made this Jesus, whom you crucified, both Lord and Christ." Peter stated boldly. He looked from person to person, making eye contact with each one, almost challenging someone to disagree.

Judith and Ethan gasped as the words took effect on them. The Christ? The Messiah? Had they seen their Messiah put to death? Watched and condoned it? Judith scanned the faces in the crowd, wondering if anyone else felt as guilty as she. Suddenly her eyes focused on a pair of brilliant brown eyes staring back at her. Reuben!

"It makes sense," Ethan whispered. "Judith, it does make sense. God sacrificed his own Son. That's why John the Baptizer called Him the Lamb of God which takes away the sins of the world. A human Passover lamb. Nothing could ever constitute as great a sacrifice or be acceptable to Jehovah."

"I can't forget that He was the cause of Jair's death," Judith replied, turning away. "I can't let go of that." They stood together in silence, trying to assimilate everything they were hearing. Suddenly Ethan gasped.

"That makes sense now too," Ethan stated quickly. "Herod was determined to kill the King of the Jews. Jesus must have been born right after the census was taken. Herod made sure they killed every baby boy." Judith's eyes opened wide in comprehension and she continued the explanation.

"If even one had been missed Herod would have fanatically searched the earth until he found him. Jair's death, in one way, secured safety for the Messiah."

"It's all clear now." Ethan pulled his wife to him as her eyes began to shine and her entire body quivered with excitement. "Praise Jehovah. Jair was sacrificed so God's son could go free."

"I remember something else. Jesus once said he was the good shepherd and would lay down his life for the sheep. Listen, Judith! He said no man could take his life from him but he had the power to lay it down and to take it again. Remember when he died? It was as if He willed His spirit to leave. If he could do that he has the power to take it up again. I believe He is alive! He is our Messiah!"

"What can we do?" Judith asked. "He was crucified and now he is alive. What can we do?" They looked up. Peter had paused.

"What shall we do then?" Ethan called out to him.

"Repent and be baptized, every one of you, in the name of Jesus Christ so that your sins may be forgiven." Ethan's arm wrapped around his wife and they moved forward towards a new understanding. The Messiah had come and touched them in more ways than one.

Judith felt another light touch on her arm. Turning, she faced Reuben. Ethan drew the boy between them and Judith gazed with love on both of them. She had a sudden vision of what lay ahead. Passover meals, garments to weave, sheep to shear. There were grandparents waiting at home for them. She looked up to see Ethan watching her.

"Do you know what the name Reuben means?" she asked, looking from Ethan to Reuben and back. "It means, *Behold, a son.*"

Breinigsville, PA USA
19 May 2010
238330BV00002B/1/P